Magical M

The Case of the
Leprechaun's Luck

Written By **Brenda Elser & Kristin Loehrmann**
Illustrated By **Rose Mary Berlin**

ACKNOWLEDGMENTS

From Brenda:

First, and always central in my life, I'd like to acknowledge my husband, Bill. I know it's a Hallmark card saying... but I really am thankful every day for the gift of your friendship and love. Your talent knows no bounds since you serve as editor, technical layout specialist, and CEO for these books. Without you they would not have existed. Thanks for believing in us and making it happen.

A big thank you to Rose Mary. We fell in love with your artistic talent but we received the gift of your creative genius as well. We feel so lucky that you are a part of these books! (It must be such a burden to be perfect.)

To our editors – Pamela - you bring out the best in our writing with just the right questions and suggestions to spur us along. Thank you for that! Karen – Your extra efforts and attention to detail will not be forgotten. And to Nicolas, our Jr. Editor, you are insightful and wise beyond your years. Thanks for giving us the kids' perspective.

And finally to Kristin, my co-author. Your creative mind adds so much beauty to our ideas. Thanks for the crazy fun!

From Kristin:

To the teachers, staff and PTSA at Carriage Crest and Lake Youngs Elementary schools in Kent, Washington. Your dedication to the profession, and the way you nurture every child humbles me, inspires me, and makes me want to write books kids want to read.

To my family, who humors me when I tell them, "Don't bother me. I'm writing."

To Brenda, whose twists and turns make each book even better than the last.

I'm honored to even take a stab at creating something as Magical as this simple thing called "A Book."

Contents

1. Dear Trickster

Eva paced the floor in her living room, wearing her usual mix of brightly colored clothes – a sturdy pair of pink hiking boots with mismatched socks and rainbow-striped leggings under a denim skirt. Her warm tan jacket and backpack were on the floor by the couch, ready for another adventure. In her hand she clutched a ransom note informing her that Lauren, her best girlfriend, had been kidnapped.

Last night they'd had a sleep-over of epic proportions: recorded themselves singing along with the radio, eaten homemade caramel popcorn until they were sick, tried on all of Eva's mother's jewelry, and fallen asleep somewhere during their third movie. When morning came, however, Eva's plans of sharing a breakfast of her mother's special pancakes (with chocolate syrup instead of maple syrup), were interrupted by this disastrous turn of events.

"Now, Eva," Mrs. O'Hare had consoled her daughter when she'd found the note, "please don't worry. I'm certain you and Robert will find Lauren in no time."

"But mom," Eva had wailed. "You said we didn't need to worry about the Tooth Fairy trying to get revenge!"

"No," Mrs. O'Hare had said gently, "what I *said* was The Board took away her flying powers. But Diva is *very* clever, and I've no doubt she had help from her... well, her *connections*. And now, you just might need a bit of help from *my* connections."

At the moment, Mrs. O'Hare stood at the bay

windows of their living room. She'd pulled the curtains open as far as they'd go to let the beautiful afternoon sunshine pour in. She'd brought in a stepladder from the hall closet and was now busy hanging tear-shaped crystals from the curtain rod so they'd catch the light. The sun's rays touched the crystals and scattered hundreds of tiny rainbows around the room; the walls and furniture danced with so much color that rainbows shined from even the farthest corners.

"We really *'Lucked out'* with such sunny weather in March," Eva's mom said from the step ladder as she hung another crystal, laughing at a joke only she seemed to get.

"Mom! This is pretty and all, but what are you doing? We're in a state of *emergency*! The Detective's Manual says you should never panic, but Lauren has been kidnapped! Kid-*Napped*, I tell you!" Eva held up the piece paper in her clenched fist and shook it for added drama. "Why are you hanging those now? And where is Robert? He should have been here already!" Eva flung herself onto the couch, pulling at her strawberry blond curls.

"I know you're worried about Lauren, dear, but trust me. She's going to be just fine." Mrs. O'Hare stepped down from the ladder after the last crystal was hung. "She hasn't even been gone a full day. But I *did* call her mother to let her know that Lauren is doing something special with us. Her family doesn't need to worry about anything while you and Robert get this straightened out."

"Doing something special? Special what? Who'd believe that?"

"It *is* special, and she *will* be with you... once you join her," Mrs. O'Hare said, giving her a stern look. "Now, quit worrying, sweetie. I just saw Robert coming up the front drive, so why don't you answer the door so you both can review the facts like serious detectives."

"Finally!" Eva shouted, exploding off the couch and rushing to the front door just as Robert knocked.

"Robert! Where have you been? Do you even

know what a crisis is?" She stepped onto the porch, shutting the door behind her, and glowered at him.

"Uh... hello to you too," Robert replied, shaking the spiky brown hair out of his eyes. "And, thank you very much, I'd be delighted to come in. *And* I know what 'crisis' means. I'm a detective, remember?" He tried to move past her into the house, but she blocked him. "Geesh, I had to pack a few things, okay? After the whole Rot Guard ordeal in Fairy Land I knew I'd better come prepared."

Robert wore jeans and boots like Eva's (not pink, of course. He considered himself a rugged outdoorsman). The backpack slung over one shoulder of his warm green jacket was so stuffed with emergency provisions that the zipper strained to contain it all.

"Eva?" Mrs. O'Hare's voice was muffled. "I thought you were in a hurry."

"You're a *junior* detective," Eva whispered to him. "And we *are* in a hurry. Wait until you hear what the note says!" She raised an eyebrow at him and moved aside. "Get ready to be amazed."

When they entered the room, they were at once splashed with hundreds of tiny rainbows.

"Whoahhh," Robert said, looking around in awe. He held out his arm to watch the colors travel and dance. "Cool…" He dropped his backpack on the floor just so he could watch the colors play across his hands.

Mrs. O'Hare smiled at him and sat on the couch. "So, children, first things first. Have a seat. As you know, a good detective always lays out the facts before anything else." She leaned forward and gestured for them to have some of the fresh fruit and milk she'd set out. Robert flopped down on a chair and grabbed for an apple slice while Eva began reviewing what had happened so far.

"Okay. One: Robert, Lauren and I went to Fairy Land after Halloween to find the candy that was stolen from all the neighborhood kids." Eva paused to reach into her back pocket and retrieve her detective notebook. She flipped through a few pages. "Two: A ghost named Stubby helped us discover it was our neighborhood Tooth Fairy, Diva, who took it. She was planning to use *our* candy to

pay her ghost employees for remodeling *her* home! Can you believe that?"

"Yeah!" Robert interrupted, "And three: You can make wishes with baby teeth, and magic is how planes fly *and* magic makes cell phones work. And four: Teachers *never* tell you this kind of stuff! There's a real problem with our educational system. I'm thinking about not going anymore!" He crunched his apple angrily, sitting back and crossing his arms with a nod.

"Robert!" Eva said turning to him, "That's not three and four! I'm reviewing the facts!"

"Dear," her mother said, "you've told me all about the key players in the heist, but the Halloween candy was returned to its rightful owners by some friends of mine so I think we can consider that case closed. Why don't you skip ahead?"

(Eva was momentarily distracted, remembering her surprise when the three of them had raced down to her basement the morning after their adventure in Fairy Land expecting to see piles of candy that the Tooth Fairy had stolen from the neighborhood. Instead, there were only piles of sparkling glitter and the lone bags of their own Halloween candy. Mrs. O'Hare had simply shrugged after they'd quizzed her about what had happened. How had the candy been returned? Instead of answers she'd handed them all brooms and had them cleaning sparkles from the basement for so long they stopped caring about what had happened – they just wished whoever did it had been a bit tidier about the 'helpful hand.')

Eva pursed her lips and gave Robert a stern 'I'm the detective in charge' look (causing Robert to give her the *'whatever'* cross-eyed, tongue-sticking-out-to-the-side look).

Flipping a few more pages in her notebook she began again. "The Tooth Fairy was planning to hold us in her gigantic tooth castle's Decaying Dungeon until she had all of our baby teeth. I think she's mad because Lauren tricked her. I guess she felt like we were breaking some kind of deal or something. But that isn't fair since the candy wasn't even hers in the first place!"

"No, dear – Diva doesn't play fair... And she *does* seem fixated on the three of you and *your* baby teeth specifically..." Mrs. O'Hare mused. "Why don't you read Robert the note you found under your pillow this morning."

Eva leaped off the couch, carefully unfolded the now very wrinkled note, and began to read, "*Dear Tricksters, I've kidnapped your friend, her baby teeth are now mine! Want to offer your teeth, perhaps as a fine? After all, you broke our contract (your lies were over the top!) So, meet me in The Land of Luck, and we can make the swap. You know who!*"

"This is beyond terrible! You know she isn't really going to give up Lauren *or* her baby teeth. She only wants us to come to her so she can have ours too!"

"My sweet girl, don't worry. With great detective skills, *and* a little Luck, there is always a way."

Robert stopped trying to catch rainbow prisms and put his apple down. "A way? What kind of way?"

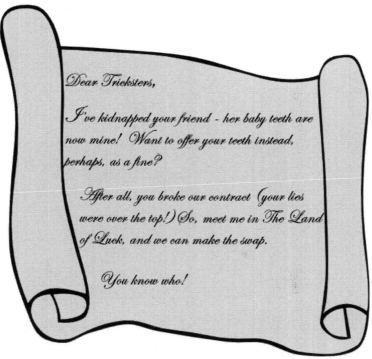

Dear Tricksters,

I've kidnapped your friend - her baby teeth are now mine! Want to offer your teeth instead, perhaps, as a fine?

After all, you broke our contract (your lies were over the top!) So, meet me in The Land of Luck, and we can make the swap.

You know who!

"What you don't realize is that there are other forms of magic," Mrs. O'Hare confided, leaning in closer. "Baby teeth aren't the only way to make wishes. I believe what you need is a Golden Coin from a Pot of Gold. Golden Coins have a bit 'O' magic that *will* work in our world."

2. Do You Believe?

Robert jumped to his feet, "Are you kidding me? This is amazing!" He pumped his fists in the air. "We're gonna be kajillionaires after all! I can't wait to tell my parents!" He sung a little off-key tune and jigged a dance that involved spinning and flailing his hands and feet.

"Mr. Adams," Eva's mom interrupted his circles, "am I to understand that you would use a Golden Coin to make yourself rich *rather* than save your friend?" She looked at her lap and began carefully smoothing her wool slacks, picking off invisible specks of lint deliberately.

Eva grinned as Robert stopped in mid-spin with one hand in the air and a foot frozen in a kick. She'd heard that tone before and you just couldn't argue with it.

He dropped his arms and legs in a slouch. "Nooo... Ahhh... Gosh, I just got a little... I just thought 'hey, what about asking for...'"

"And no, Mr. Adams, before you ask, you may *not* use the wish to have a million more wishes," she continued. "That's what makes each Coin so special. Only one wish per Coin."

Robert flopped back down on his chair. "Of *course*, I want Lauren back."

"Mom, when are you going to tell me about how you know all this stuff?"

"Soon dear, but not today," she smiled. "Today, you have a friend to rescue." Here she paused, "I try to leave the magical issues to your father these days, but you know I'm happy to give some advice from time to time. And now my advice to you is that you collect a Golden Coin from The Land of Luck. You can use it to save Lauren by wishing all of you away from Diva and safely back home."

"Sweeet!" Robert whispered. "I knew we'd be going on another adventure!"

"The Land of Luck? What Land of Luck?" Eva's eyes widened as her mother walked toward the hallway. "Mom, where do we find the Coin? Where are we going?"

"I've put a crystal in your backpack, dear," Mrs. O'Hare said simply, walking out of the room.

"Wait! Where are you going? Aren't you at least going to tell us how we get there?" Eva jumped up from her chair and clasped her hands together pleadingly.

"You've done this on your own before," Mrs. O'Hare said, leaning briefly back into the room. "But the real question you want to ask yourselves is 'Do I believe in the Blarney?'"

Then she was gone again. The children could hear her humming to herself as she walked down the hall toward the kitchen.

"Your mom is so cool!" Robert whispered.

"She's probably getting something from the kitchen to help us. She'll be right back." Eva cleared her throat and put her hands behind her back in the manner all great detectives did in order to pace. "What do you suppose she means by 'Do you believe in the Blarney?'" she asked, using her best detective interrogation voice.

"Well that *is* a very good question, madam," Robert said imitating Eva's pacing. "Let us ask ourselves what is Blarney? And what is it about this Blarney we must believe in?" He stroked his chin thoughtfully and pretended to chomp on a pipe the way he'd seen Sherlock Holmes do in all the movies.

Eva wasn't sure, but she suspected Robert was making fun of her detective skills.

"Do *you* believe?" Robert continued, placing

one arm behind his back and pacing away from her. "Because I think, or, as one might say, I believe in the Blarney!" On this last statement he stomped his foot directly down onto one of the mini rainbows shining on the living room floor.

Immediately a burst of Golden glitter exploded into the room in a cyclone and whirled around Robert.

It was anchored to the rainbow he had just stomped upon while the top of it spun around the room throwing small objects in its path. Eva felt the wind from the twister pulling at her hair and clothes. Her mouth opened in an 'O' of amazement as Robert was lifted into the air in the middle of the spinning storm. His howls of surprise and fear faded in and out like a siren as he spun, until both he and the tornado were sucked down into the small rainbow on the floor. They were gone with a 'pop,' and not even a single Golden sparkle remained as proof of what had just happened.

Eva didn't even realize she'd been moving away until her back bumped against the wall, startling her. She took a deep breath and looked around the wind-tossed room. "Well... By deductive reasoning I'd say Robert has found the way to The Land of

Luck..."

She gathered her courage and looked around once more before deciding that perhaps she'd try touching a rainbow on the wall when she said the magic words. Maybe she'd stand a better chance of *walking* into the magical Land instead of *falling* into it the way they did with the Halloween vine in their last adventure.

"Mom! I'm going!" She picked up their backpacks and coats. "Umph! Geesh, Robert! What did you put in your pack?" she huffed, carrying their supplies to the rainbow she'd chosen.

"Do your best, dear. And be back before dark!" Her mother's voice was faint from the direction of the kitchen.

"Aw, drat!" Eva whispered, standing up as straight as she could with all the equipment she was carrying. She tapped the rainbow shining on the wall and said, "I believe in the Blarney!"

But it was impossible to avoid stepping on the

hundreds of other rainbows reflected all over the floor. So it only stood to reason that she'd been standing on one... And it was immediately clear Golden cyclones preferred *ground* transport, because it rose up from the floor, anchored to the rainbow her foot was touching.

Eva squealed and tried to keep her balance but the whirlwind easily lifted her up and spun her until she thought she was going to be sick. Blasts of Golden Dust stuck to her body as she twirled, and she held onto their backpacks as tightly as she could while the wind pulled at her.

"This must be what it's like to be caught in a real tornado!" Eva thought, starting to panic. "I... I can't... hold on to the backpacks much longer!" she cried out.

As soon as she uttered the words, the wind began to slow, and when it came to a stop, Eva found herself floating in the still air. She slowly opened her eyes to find the hush of violet, the shock of yellow, the cool of green.

All of the rainbow's colors washed over her in complete peace.

Just then, like her fall from the Halloween vine, a bright blue hole opened up, exposing the sky, and Eva was abruptly hurtled through it to the soft ground below. She tumbled head over heels across clover-filled grass, and when her acrobatic roll finally stopped, the colors were gone and she was lying face down in the greenest field she had ever seen... Or tasted... Her stomach told her that she still felt the effects of the tornado, so she decided to remain still until her dizziness subsided.

"Are you dead, Eva?" she heard from the bush beside her. She held her head and sat up just as Robert leapt from behind the shrub and shouted, "Finally!"

Eva screamed and crab-walked backward.

"What!" Robert laughed, crossing his arms, "It's just me, silly. Welcome to The Land of Luck!" He threw his arms out and gestured around them with an ear-splitting grin.

3. Reese

"How would I have known it was you?" Eva gasped, "Have you seen yourself?" She looked down at her clothes, "Correction – have you seen *us*?"

The children looked like they had been painted with Gold. It coated their bodies from head to toe making them look like living statues. "What *is* this stuff?" Eva asked staggering to her feet and trying to wipe some of it off.

"Oh, don't bother trying to get it off. I've

been trying for the last five minutes, waiting for you, and it's stuck. I mean *really* stuck! It must be from that crazy Golden tornado. See?" He showed her the method he'd been using unsuccessfully, when suddenly he stopped. "Hey, great! You remembered our packs! Let's try taking it off with some of the water I brought." Robert unzipped his pack, and Halloween candy spilled out onto the clover as he rummaged.

"You brought candy?" Eva said with a smirk, crossing her arms. "Is that a part of our emergency equipment?"

"Uh, if you'll recall, it came in pretty handy for our Dungeon escape." He poured water into his hands and scrubbed them together.

And scrubbed some more. And then just a little more.

Eva stood up and rubbed her hands together to show Robert how a real professional did things.

She grimaced and tried a little harder. Still

nothing came off. "Well, this is completely ridiculous! It must come off somehow." Eva looked at her Golden hands and trailed off, "Unless... Do you think everyone here is this color?"

"How would I know?" Robert shrugged. "I've only been here five minutes longer than you." He grinned, "But hey! If we're in trouble we can pretend we're statues. No one will even notice us!" He struck an Egyptian pose by sticking his hands out in either direction with one foot up in the air.

Eva giggled. It wasn't a very Junior Detective-like thing to do but she couldn't help herself. He did look like a statue covered in all that Gold.

"Look Eva, I'm a fountain," he said sucking some water into his mouth and blowing it in a stream into the air.

Not to be outdone, Eva leapt up and tried to show off her own pose. "Hey, do I look like an angel?" she asked putting her hands together as if she were in prayer.

"Hardly," Robert answered. "It's more like this," he demonstrated with his hands outstretched. "You have to put your hands out wide, like you're hugging the whole world. Or bringing some kind of news or something."

The children were having so much fun they didn't notice another person had joined them.

"Actually, it's probably closer to this," said a blond girl about their age. She held her hands up and made her mouth a perfect little 'O.' "They're always singing about something, and they're super proud about it so they raise their hands like 'Hey, look at me. I'm singing here.'"

Robert choked on a sip of water, and Eva let out a 'yip' and spun around wielding the karate-chop hands she'd learned in her martial arts class. (She had convinced her mother that learning self-defense was "absolutely essential" to being a detective.)

The girl stood a few feet away, her hands still in mid-air. Her long blond hair curled from beneath her Peter Pan style hat, and the children could plainly see the tips of her pointed ears. Her long skirt and leather boots would probably have been as forest green as her tunic if they weren't covered with Gold dust.   Her rosy cheeks reminded Eva of Lauren.

"What are you doing? My name's Reese. What's yours? How long did it take you to collect all of that Luck? I've never seen anyone with as much Luck as you two. You must have started collecting before the shortage. Are you here for the Tournament?"

The children gawked at the girl, who asked as many questions as Robert, and whose bright blue eyes watched them intently. When Reese smiled at them, dimples appeared in both cheeks. Eva was silent for a moment before she finally remembered she was in charge and she should probably say something.

"Uh, hi... I'm Eva and that's Robert." Robert, who had fallen to the ground coughing as he choked on his sip of water, greeted Reese with a wave of one hand, pounding his chest with his other.

Reese continued to smile, as the children stared at her mutely. Each seemed to be waiting for the other to speak.

Finally Reese said, "What's up with your hands there?"

Eva looked down at her self-defense pose and quickly put her hands on her hips.

"Uh, karate. You should be more careful startling people... I could have hurt you." Reese threw her head back and laughed, and Eva felt her face redden as Robert snickered also.

She shot him a withering look and crossed her arms over her chest. "Anyway, we're sort of new here."

Robert stood up and fake karate chopped in Eva's direction, still snorting. "What do you mean how did we collect all of the Luck?"

Reese had grown serious trying to imitate the way Eva had positioned her hands. She looked up and smiled broadly at her new friends. "If you're so new here how did you collect so much? With as much Gold as you're wearing, it looks like you've been saving it up *forever*."

Robert and Eva looked down at themselves. Was that what that Gold stuff was? Luck? "I, uh, I don't know," Eva stammered, unsure if they should tell Reese about the cyclone or not.

"You *do* know they'd never let an outsider win the Golden Coin and become our leader, right?" Reese dropped her hands and tilted her head.

"Did you just say Golden Coin?"

"Yes. You win a Golden Coin in the Tournament if you make it to the end of the course without using all your Luck. Then, after you're presented with the Golden Coin, you become a Leader of the Land for the next ten years." Reese stopped. "Is he okay?" she nodded her head toward Robert who was chopping the air and whispering, "Hah! Hiiiiyah! Hah!"

"Yeah, sometimes his funny bone acts up and it makes him weird," Eva said, kicking a little dirt at him with her shoe to make him stop.

"What?" he demanded dropping his hands and pushing Eva gently. "We don't know about any Tournament, Reese. We're here on an urgent case to save our friend *and* the world at large from a kray kray ex-tooth fairy!" He rotated a finger around one of his ears. "Crazy," he whispered.

"I don't understand. How could you not hear about the Tournament? Everyone in the known universe has heard of it. How far out of town do you live? What do you mean kray kray tooth fairy?" Reese paused her battery of questions and looked at them closely. "*Who* are you again? And why are your ears *round*?"

4. Danger's My Middle Name

"Robert, as usual you skipped over everything!" Eva scolded. "Reese, I'm sorry my friend is being so ruuude."

"Hey!" Robert scowled at her.

"I can explain everything," she said walking toward Reese with her hand extended to shake. "But we could really use some directions. Do you think you can help us?"

"I suppose," Reese said grasping Eva's hand. "Are you walking to the main village? That's where the starting line is. It isn't as far away as it looks. We can talk on the way 'cause the Tournament starts soon. Grab your backpacks."

Eva and Robert hurried behind Reese as she led them to a road spanning two rolling hills in more shades of green than they ever thought existed. Off in the distance, nestled in a valley, they could see a medieval castle sitting in the middle of a small town.

"It's beautiful," Eva breathed, stopping to stare at the castle. "I can't believe I'm actually seeing this."

"Whoooah," Robert's mouth hung open.

"You two *are* new if you've never seen the capitol of The Land of Luck before," Reese guided them along the smooth cobbled stones. "But you really must tell me how you have so much Golden Luck all over you. Especially since we've had a massive shortage recently."

"A massive Luck shortage?" Eva asked.

"It started a couple of days ago and we don't

know why. Normally my people can collect Luck by letting the Golden Dust build up the way it's collected on you." She pointed to the Gold Dust on Eva's hands. "Everyone here uses the magic of Luck every day to... well, to do *everything*, so we don't usually have much of it on us unless we're preparing for a Tournament."

"I don't get it," Robert said. "And this stuff doesn't feel very Lucky to me! Actually, it feels a bit sticky..."

"Of course it's sticky! You wouldn't want it falling off before you had a chance to use it would you?" Reese laughed. "I don't think I've ever met anyone who doesn't know about Luck. Every land uses it!"

"We can *use* this Luck?" Robert said examining his hands and arms.

"Sure, but I'd hold onto it if I were you... I mean, if you still plan to join the Tournament now that you know you can't be our leader."

"Oh, no, no – we don't need to be in the

Tournament. We're not here to be leaders. We just need a Golden Coin to save our friend," Eva said. "Can you tell us where we can get one of those? Then we'll just head back home and leave you to your pick-a-leader thingy."

"You can't just *get* a Golden Coin!" Reese laughed, stopping to lean over for a good knee-slapping chuckle. "Golden Coins are special. It's the only thing we make with the help of everyone in our society. We don't normally use teamwork to get things done." Here Reese shook her head before continuing. "They're so special that if any extra Coins *are* made they're collected in a Pot attached to a rainbow. We save them for emergencies. You can make *any* wish with them, you know. But the rainbow's protected by a spell that never allows anyone to get close unless you're a Leader of the Land."

"Yes! We know about rainbows! Oh, my gosh, Eva – we *were* taught something about magic in school!" Robert hooted. "So, what's the big deal with making it all the way through to the end still covered in this sticky Luck stuff?" Robert reached up and tried to rub his face clean with his shirt sleeve when Reese stopped him.

"The *big deal* is that if someone has the most 'sticky Luck stuff' at the end, they prove they can solve problems with their wit and not by Luck alone. I competed in the last Tournament but I didn't make it to the end. This time I know what I'm up against, and I'm ready! This year I *will* earn a Golden Coin and join the other leaders. Then I'll be able to teach my people the value of teamwork!"

"The Tournament is the *only* way to get a Coin?" Eva asked, scribbling in her notebook as they walked.

"Yup. I think I mentioned they're very special, right?"

"Hey, if you tried out for this Tournament before, and they only hold these contests every ten years, how old *are* you?" Robert stepped in front of Reese and looked at her more closely. He put his hands on his hips and said, "I'm nine!"

Reese watched him stand to his full height and try to look down his nose at her (even though she was just the tiniest bit taller than him). Trying not to giggle, she said, "We age differently here. I *am* fairly young to compete, but I'm not as young as you are!" She stepped forward, almost touching Robert's nose, and stared back at him. "In The Land of Luck I'm ten."

Robert blushed and said, "Well, I'll be ten in a couple of months!"

"Robert! You're always taking us off track," Eva sighed. "I'm sorry, Reese, but we really have to figure out how to get a Golden Coin and save our friend. Can you help us?"

Reese side-stepped Robert so she could keep walking. "Why don't you tell me what happened to your friend and then I'll be able to tell you if I can help."

"*'In The Land of Luck I'm ten'...*" Robert sneered to himself as trudged behind the girls.

Eva began to share with Reese their adventure in Fairy Land. As they walked through fields and thickets, she told her of Lauren's bravery and how the three of them had solved the case of the Halloween candy stolen from their neighborhood.

By the time Eva was finished telling their tale, the three children had arrived at the edge of the quaint town surrounding the castle. Reese paused so Eva and Robert could take in their surroundings. Pubs, tea shops and pea patches dotted the landscape. Stone and wood structures with thatched roofs lined cobbled streets just like all the medieval towns they had read about in story books. Off in the distance they could hear the sounds of music and a large gathering muted by the sloping hillside.

"Of course, we must rescue your friend! I'll do everything I can to help. This is my mission! It's what I want to teach my people when I'*m* a leader. We must hold friendship above Luck and work together as a society! Unfortunately, I can only think of one way to get the Golden Coin you'll need to wish your friend to safety and all of you back home." She grabbed Eva's hand and said, "You'll have to join me in the Tournament." The children nodded at her, not entirely certain what they were agreeing with. "I should warn you," she continued. "It's dangerous. Contestants have died trying to make it through some of the obstacles."

"A good detective always completes her case. No matter what," Eva said with only the slightest tremble in her voice. "Besides, we have to save Lauren."

"Yeah. And Danger is my middle name," Robert agreed.

"Your middle name is Hugo," Eva said.

"Hugo?" Reese asked.

"She meant *Hero*. My middle name is Hero." He glared at Eva.

"Wow," Reese said. "That's good news. We'll certainly need a hero to get past the obstacles and win the Golden Coin. But you're both going to need to cover up a bit. My people will be suspicious of how much Luck you have during the shortage. It could cause a riot. And now we'd better hurry. The Tournament will be starting soon."

5. The Weight of Luck

The children held hands tightly as they made their way through the throng. It had grown warm as they walked through the crowd, and Eva wished they could ditch their coats, but Reese had encouraged them to stay covered or someone would notice how much Luck the children had, and the crowd could become dangerous. Everywhere they turned, men and women were proudly cloaked in various amounts of Gold and green.

"Hey!" Robert hooted. "I'm taller than everyone here... Practically!"

Eva nodded, looking around as they walked.

At last they came to a large rainbow-colored balloon arch spanning the wide cobbled street. The banner read "Leader's Tournament Starting Line."

"Come on! We register over there. It's going to start any minute and we still need a plan to get across the acid river and past the troll." Reese motioned them toward some long tables assembled along the side of the street.

Eva and Robert gave her the thumbs-up and two gigantic fake smiles, determined not to let her see how the words "acid river" and "troll" had terrified them. Still holding hands, (though now more tightly), Eva marched faster, feeling Robert's arm growing stiffer as they walked. Finally, when it felt like she was dragging a small tree stump behind her she stopped and glared at him.

"Robert! Stop pulling! A second ago, you said you were a hero."

"I'm not scared if that's what you think," his

voice quivered. "I'm just... Well, aren't you a little *concerned* about acid? And a troll? A *troll*, Eva!"

Reese shouted again, waving her hands to let them know she'd saved them a place in line. People bumped around the children, trying to ensure they had a good starting spot.

"Listen," Eva said as softly as she could over the din. "Trolls are... well, they're like the Rot Guards from Fairy Land, right?" Robert nodded, brightening just a bit.

"And how many times have we put the couch cushions and pillows on the floor and made a trail to the kitchen?"

Robert interrupted, "...So we don't get eaten by the alligators!"

Eva nodded. Although they were much wiser and more *mature* now that they were detectives, she felt it was necessary to remind him about the game they used to play when they were *young*.

"We have plenty of training for this!" she

encouraged him. "Even though we knew that if we stepped on the floor it was just the floor – not real alligators – we played the game like we might lose a leg if we messed up. This is just the same. Geesh, for all we know, the acid river here is some kind of soda or something."

"Yeah, yeah! Soda!" Robert nodded. "I think you're right, Eva." He stood taller and nodded again. "I mean, I would have probably figured that out on my own, but thanks for your, uh, assistance."

Eva rolled her eyes at him. She was still terrified but she knew her little speech had calmed him down when he grabbed her hand even tighter and began to hustle her to the spot where Reese waited for them.

"Finally!" Reese said, exasperated. "You took so long, I thought you might have decided your friend wasn't important enough to rescue!" Eva looked hurt and Robert looked indignant. But before either of them could protest, Reese continued, "Now let's get this show on the road! The contest is going to start any minute and there's a long line for Luck Weight!"

She shoved them toward a long table where several volunteers in standard hunter green garb efficiently handled paperwork. Each contestant filled in his or her registration sheet and handed it to a volunteer who whisked it away. They were then directed to a large scale that read "Luck-O-Meter." Eva and Robert watched as a contestant stood on the scale and the arrow twanged to 25%. When the volunteer had registered the contestant's Luck Weight, the next contestant moved forward to be weighed.

"What's that?" Eva whispered.

"We measure how much Luck a contestant has at the beginning of the race and then compare it to the amount at the end. Only one contestant can win, and sometimes more than one makes it across the finish line, so the one who has the most Luck left is the winner."

Eva and Robert nodded gravely. Only one

person could win a Coin and they were competing against all of these contestants?

They moved forward in the registration line anxiously. The line moved quickly through the almost-endless line of contestants but came to a screeching halt once Eva and Robert made it to the front.

"Wh... where... wh..." the green-clad man fumbled, staring at Robert's head and ears.

Robert grinned broadly and said, "Hiya. I'm Robert." He stuck his hand out as if to introduce himself formally. The man tapped his co-worker vigorously and Robert smiled at him, pretending not to notice. "I'm kinda new here, so I'm not 'zackly sure what to do, but I can follow directions like a pro."

Now both volunteers stared at them silently.

Finally Robert said, "Uh... Cannn yooou heeear meee?"

By now the other volunteers had begun to talk amongst themselves about the two spectacles that claimed to be "new in town." Quiet whispers and serious nods made Robert and Eva feel very self-conscious until Reese stepped in front of the children and said loudly, "Yes, that's right. Their ears are... well, funny..." The men hushed. She turned to the children and whispered, "No offense..."

"None taken," Robert held up his hand and Eva nodded again, slightly dazed.

Reese took the pen from the volunteer's hand and said, "Here, let me help you."

She handed the pen to Robert, who signed the registration form and passed the pen to Eva.

After Eva signed her form, Reese took their papers and moved them to the drop box where all the others had been collected. She reviewed the billboard where contestants had been assigned numbers, and after punching a few bits of information into the system, she grabbed the two tickets that spit out of a gigantic clunky contraption.

She handed each child a number and said,

"Since you're not wearing hats, we'll have to pin this on your shirts." The volunteers had quieted altogether now, simply staring as both Robert and Eva removed their jackets and awkwardly tied them around their waists. Then Reese pushed them toward the Luck-O-Meter and told Robert to stand on the scale.

As Robert's weight settled, lights and alarms began to scream and blink and whirl. Sirens sounded as the arrow bounced on "100% Luck! 100% Luck!" again and again. Now *everyone* in the crowd became silent and stared at the newcomers.

"Why is everyone staring at us?" Eva gulped, looking around at all the angry expressions.

"Well…" Reese said matter-of-factly, pinning the numbers to their shirts. "We've never, *ever* seen this much Luck on a contestant before. And since there's a shortage, people are probably a bit suspicious. But mainly I suppose it's because you're, uh… Well… you're human."

"So?" Robert snorted.

"Well, *we're* Leprechauns, silly!" Reese grinned.

6. No Humans

It was Eva and Robert's turn to stare at Reese and the rest of the Leprechauns in the crowd. "Land of Luck! Duh!" Robert smacked his head and grinned at Eva. "Of course they're Leprechauns! And they're not green! And they're our size!"

"Yeah, and you're almost as tall as some of them," Eva snickered.

The clatter of a single pen dropping echoed across the vast stone courtyard. The volunteers had even stopped shuffling their papers as they continued to stare.

"Uh, stop talking Robert..." She cautioned, looking at all the angry eyes focused on them. "We *are* human. So?"

The collective buzz grew louder, and the children spun around sizing up the gathering mob. But instead of an attack, a paper airplane soared over the heads of the crowd and with perfect 'Luck' it landed on Robert's head and stuck in his spiky hair, looking almost like a ladies' small hat.

Reese reached out and plucked the plane from his hair and unfolded it. She read the note and grimaced. "Okay, 94-O'Sweeney," she grumbled the contestant's entry code. "What's the meaning of this?"

Someone shouted from the crowd, "No humans!"

Soon the others began to chant, "No humans! No humans! No humans!"

Eva assumed a karate pose and Robert clenched his fists as Reese aimed a grim look toward the volunteer's table. "Well?" she demanded. "Aren't you going to do anything about this?"

They looked at each other, dumbfounded. One of them turned and mumbled, "I'll go get the manual to see what should be done."

But the crowd looked like it was growing quickly, and if it didn't stop soon there may be a complete riot. More Leprechauns began chanting "No humans!" Soon they had formed a circle around the three friends. A few contestants even jumped forward and gave Eva and Robert a small push before running back into the safety of the crowd.

Finally Reese had had enough. She leapt up onto one of the long tables and shouted, "Leprechauns! My fellow Leprechauns! Listen to me!"

It took some yelling but when she finally had their attention, Reese stood with her hands on her hips and glared. Her pointed ears glowed bright red with anger. "You are all simply upset because of the amount of Luck they have. Maybe you're worried it gives them an unfair advantage, but if you knew why they're here, perhaps you'd choose to work together and help them as a team! Their goal is honorable – to help a friend – and we can learn from them!"

The crowd was completely silent until someone yelled, "That's not the Leprechaun way! We have our Luck and our wits to pull us through and we don't need to change! *Or* help any outsiders!"

Reese fumed as the Leprechauns moved toward Eva and Robert. The children heard her whisper something before she raised her hand to her lips and breathed lightly as if blowing a kiss to the crowd. A gentle mist of Golden Dust settled across the mob, and in an instant everyone calmed and seemed to be in better spirits. Robert tapped Eva and pointed at Reese to make sure she'd seen it too.

"She got some of that Luck stuff off by blowing on it!"

"Yeah! She used it to calm everyone down."

The crowd began to murmur again, but now they seemed to be talking about plans to make it through the obstacles instead of how to eliminate Eva and Robert, and the group that had gathered around them began to wander back toward the rainbow balloons as if all was forgotten.

"Don't mind them," Reese said, stepping down from the table. "This will all blow over once the competition starts."

Robert slapped his knee. "Blow over!" he shouted. "Get it? *Blow* over? As in Reese *blew* some of that Lucky Dust on the crowd? Anyone? Anyone?" He held his hand up for a high five.

Eva rolled her eyes at him and turned to Reese. "Thanks," she said, touching their new friend on the shoulder.

"Not a wise decision, young lass," a stout Leprechaun interrupted them, shaking his head at Reese. "Wasting precious magic on that stunt to quiet the crowd is careless of ye.

Simply careless. Ye should have let them throw the humans out of town. They can't win the Tournament anyway. Humans cannot be leaders of the land and ye know it."

The lone Leprechaun, O'Sweeney, growled at

Reese as he swaggered toward them. O'Sweeney was thick and tall for a Leprechaun. He was covered up to his neck in Golden Dust but his hair and beard were a flaming bright red, and he stood out in the crowd.

"You're awfully confident for a little guy," Robert snorted.

O'Sweeney's chest swelled out and his eyes were defiant as he wheeled around to face Robert. "Ye dare to make fun of yer elders?" he said. "And yeee!" he pointed at Reese, "Ye waste yer magic on these... these *humans*?" He spat the words at her. "I'd say this is a perfect example of why ye should never be a leader! Yer too young to know that humans aren't worth the bother! They find a penny and they call it 'good Luck!' They break a mirror and they call it 'bad Luck!' They don't know that Luck is earned through hard work! The *only* human who ever understood was 'The Great Kathleen.'"

A few people in the crowd stopped to listen

again when he mentioned the name 'The Great Kathleen'.

"Hey," Robert nudged Eva and whispered. "Isn't Kathleen your mom's name?"

Eva nodded and continued to listen.

"See?" Reese quietly replied shaking her head at O'Sweeney. "You said it yourself. Not all humans are worthless Luck scavengers. Why don't you give these two a chance? All they want is to bring their friend back…"

"*Do* share…" O'Sweeney said sarcastically. "We're *all ears!*"

The Leprechauns hooted with laughter and Robert leaned in close to Eva. "Get it? Get it?" he said. "All ears! As in *pointed ears!*" He pointed to his ears and then to O'Sweeney's sharp ear lobes. Eva scowled at him, but Robert just grinned wider and slapped his knee.

"Oy! Listen up!" Reese shouted again and the crowd stopped laughing.

As she wove the tale of her two new friends, Robert and Eva noted Reese embellished a few points (which was fine with both of them, as it moved the crowd to tearful sympathy for their human competitors), and left out others (which was also fine with the children, as the Leprechauns did not need to know anything about Robert's misadventures with the Tooth Fairy's white furnishings).

O'Sweeney took a deep breath. "Well, well…" He appeared to be quite interested in his shoes, and he did not look up to meet their eyes.

"See," said Reese, "not everything is as it appears. Maybe you could even help us."

O'Sweeney cleared his throat and shuffled his feet. "That's not the Leprechaun way," he gruffed. Then he straightened up and shook a finger at them, "I'm not just going to hand over my chance to win the Gold Coin. I've worked too hard for this!"

"We're not looking for a free ride," Eva said, quickly squeezing Robert's hand before he could complain. (Because, of course, if it was free, Robert wanted it.) "We just want to do our best and bring our friend home – where she belongs."

O'Sweeney raised his eyes and took a close look at Eva, searching her face for a moment before his features softened. He took Eva's hand and said, "Ye know, ye do remind me of The Great Kathleen just a wee bit. I see it in yer eyes." He smiled so that only the corners of his mouth turned up slightly.

"By any chance," Eva began and stopped. It was almost too strange to ask him the question she was thinking. It would be a long-shot, and she didn't want O'Sweeney to think she was crazy.

"Come, come, what is it?" he asked. "Ye'd best make it fast. The race is going to begin in a blink."

Eva began again, "By any chance... Is The Great Kathleen's last name... is it O'Hare?"

O'Sweeney's eyes lit up. "Nope!" he laughed.

"It was Warfield."

Suddenly a bell clanged and the band began to play, signaling that the race had begun. O'Sweeney abruptly dropped Eva's hand, gave them a salute and a wink and raced off into the crowd.

Eva gave a shaky laugh. How silly to think he might have been talking about her mother. There was no way her mother could have been this Great Kathleen... Right?

7. Not Nice

"Miss?" A volunteer grabbed Eva's sleeve before they could join the mass of contestants at the starting line. "The bell has sounded and your Luck must be weighed if you're going to join the contest."

"Of course, of course," Reese agreed, hurrying Eva toward the Luck-O-Meter. Maybe it was because of the Golden Dust Reese had blown over the crowd or maybe it was because the race had already started, but this time no one stopped or seemed to care that the sirens and whistles sounded again when Eva measured

'100% Luck!'

Instead, the crowd of contestants jostled each other and pushed the children forward as they joined the mass of Leprechauns on a course that would be long and treacherous, testing each one's abilities to rely on their skills and wit. The single winner would be leader of The Land of Luck for the next decade, so every Leprechaun took the contest very seriously and had trained rigorously for the event.

Reese, Eva and Robert trotted shoulder to shoulder with their competitors, following the red flags that marked the obstacle course. "So!" Robert shouted to Eva above the noisy crowd and music, even though they were just six inches from each other. "Our backpacks are full of useful items that should help us win this thing in a jiffy."

Eva looked doubtful. "Should!" she shouted back. "If by 'win' you mean 'not die in a river of acid!' And if by 'jiffy' you mean 'be home by dark' – like my mom said!"

Robert hooted and punched Eva's arm. "That's the spirit," he shouted. "Besides! You said the river was soda!" Eva rolled her eyes at him.

The crowd had formed a well-organized line in the street and was quickly winding out of the village into the meadow beyond the castle. Strolling bands played music around them as they walked, and friends and family members waved from the sidewalks, threw flowers, and yelled encouragement to each of the contestants as they passed. Scattered confetti fell like rain, and the arch of balloons, which had been severed when the starting bell sounded, now floated in the breeze. It was so festive the excitement vibrated in the air.

Once they had passed the cobbled stone streets into the countryside, Reese scouted the landscape they walked, making sure they steered clear of the better known tricksters in the pack. There were a few who were famous for wasting others' precious time convincing them to exhaust their hard-earned Luck.

"I've told you it's unheard of..." Reese said thoughtfully, "this 'sticking together' strategy. If we make it, this could really change the Leprechaun way..."

"You worry too much," Robert laughed, turning away from them and trotting toward a Leprechaun a few paces ahead. "Hello, fellow competitor!" he grinned.

The Leprechaun had snatched a blue balloon and was holding the string tightly. He waved Robert away with his free hand.

"*Ahem*! I said 'Hellooo!'" Robert repeated.

Without slowing, the Leprechaun said, "Hello yerself. Now be gone with ye."

Robert frowned. "Not nice."

"Tell ye' what," the Leprechaun said, hustling around a fallen log. "Let's the two of us have a lovely cup o' tea at the old stone quarry, and we'll get to know each other."

"Really?" Robert brightened.

"No. Now be gone with ye."

Eva laughed as she caught up with them. A good detective would know how to handle a situation like this. She'd just have to use her 'good cop' interrogation skills.

She bumped Robert out of the way and said, "Hi! Cool balloon. Did you catch it in town?"

The Leprechaun looked at her sideways and broke into a jog. "It's my balloon! Ye can't have it!"

"I... Wait up! I don't want your silly balloon!"

The Leprechaun stopped suddenly, causing the children to bump right into him.

"Oop, sorry," Eva said, watching the Leprechaun carefully readjust his hat.

He held his hand up to keep Eva at arm's length. "What do ye want with an old man like me then? Come come! Make it snappy! I've a contest t' win here."

"Oh... I just thought we could share some ideas to get through the first obstacle. We're new in town. But then, I guess you knew that…" she trailed off.

"Are ye sayin' work *together*?" the Leprechaun laughed and looked at Reese with disdain. "No. And now, I bid ye farewell."

Turning to leave, he suddenly paused and appeared to reconsider. "Wait, I s'pose I should tell ye," he smiled with feigned sincerity. "The path ye want t' take is that-a-way. Most Leprechauns follow the marked flags, but if ye go yonder the other way it'll get ye past the Troll." He jabbed a stubby finger in the opposite direction of the marked path.

Eva eyed him seriously. "Can we also avoid the river if we go that way?"

"Oh, yes, yes!" the Leprechaun said. "That is definitely the way!"

"The troll too? If we go that way, we'll skip the whole troll thing?" Robert asked.

"Oh, yes, yes!" he nodded, glancing sideways at Reese who had now joined them.

She shook her head at him, but he saluted with a wink and turned on his heel, still clutching his blue balloon as if it were a life preserver.

"Wait," Robert said with a frown. "Why are you going that way? You told us to go this way."

The little man bumped his pack over his shoulder. "Ye have yer plan - I have my plan! Let me be, already!" he grimaced, tromping off toward the river.

"Well, good Luck to you then!" Robert slung his backpack over his shoulder again. "May the best man win!"

"The best *competitor*," Eva corrected him. "May the best *competitor* win." She scowled, gathering her own backpack.

Reese watched as the man disappeared over the hill. "You do realize he's a scammer, right?" she shook her head.

"Scammer?" Eva wrinkled her nose. "What do you mean?"

"I mean he lied to you," Reese said.

"Yes, we *know* what 'scammer' means. I just wondered why you'd think that. He seemed like a perfectly nice man," Robert said.

She laughed. "He *is* a very nice man. But I know my father, and *that* was a lie!"

8. Ticked Off Troll

It didn't matter that Eva and Robert weren't sure how to react, because Reese continued talking, seemingly unaware of their shock. "My mum always says, 'Yer Da wasn't like this when I married 'im.' But then he always tells her, 'Yes, I was. Ye just didn't know I was such a creative talker then.' Reese laughed and continued. "Most Leprechaun families are pretty big, but I'm an only child... Sometimes I think if I'd had a brother or sister we'd work together to win the Tournament."

"Is that why you're helping us?" Robert

asked. "Am I like the brother you never had?"

"If Reese had had a brother like you she would agree with the Leprechaun way and want to be left alone." Eva snorted. "You, my friend, are a wild card."

Reese laughed, "You two are a hoot! I don't care what they say about humans – I think you're a lot of fun. Now, come on. We're almost to the river."

The children could hear it sizzle and pop as they drew closer. When they rounded the bend, the terrifying river appeared in front of them. Its bright purple acid flowed furiously while lavender bubbles foamed and popped on the surface. Rocks on the shoreline smoked and broke apart where the river surged and touched them.

Several contestants were spread out from the edge of the river, and each one seemed to be thinking about how to make it safely across.

"Hey, there's a bridge! Why didn't you tell us

that?" Robert grumbled.

"Shhh!" Reese cautioned, pulling them behind a tree. "Just watch for a second."

Sure enough, a contestant was sneaking up to cross the bridge. His footsteps were silent and he carefully placed his feet in what appeared to be a very deliberate sequence. The children watched as he paused at the first stone step and gathered his breath. Suddenly he broke into a run so fast you would have thought his pants were on fire.

In fact, his life depended on his speed, because when he hit mid-span, a massive green arm swiftly reached out and nabbed the running Leprechaun by his Golden shirt, lifting him straight into the air. The little man's feet kept running even as he lifted his hands to his mouth and blew.

When the Leprechaun's Golden Luck cloud billowed around him, the children strained to see as the clawed fingers lost their grip. The screaming contestant hit the ground running (as the saying goes) and the Troll roared his frustration. Eva stifled a scream when she saw him rise up from his hiding place under the bridge and make a second grab for his lost meal.

The Troll was as big as a house even with half of his body still standing in the purple acid. His green muscular torso bulged from the crude woven vest he wore. His claws were as bright as red nail polish, and his jaw thrust out in an underbite that displayed the rows of his pointed teeth. Warts covered his flat nose and patches of hair sprouted across his head. In short, he was huge, ugly, and *terrifying*.

"Well *that* explains why no one uses the bridge," Robert whispered nervously.

"Yup," Reese pointed. "That contestant probably used up almost half of his Luck on this obstacle alone. We need to reach that tree line on the other side of the river to be out of the Troll's grasp." They watched as the now-slippery contestant ran along the trees, far enough away that the Troll could no longer reach him from the bridge. "We better come

up with a plan," she said reaching into her contestant's packet and pulling out a map.

"What?" Eva's eyes widened. "I thought you already had a plan!"

"Yeah, my plan was to run across the bridge."

Reese studied the map to avoid their eyes. "But in light of what we just saw, I think it's wise to change things up a bit. After all, the troll has pretty much seen it all. This is what he *does*. He's got to feed his family some way too…"

"Ewww…" Eva said. "He *eats* Leprechauns?"

Reese nodded, reaching into her pack.

Robert hopped up and down on his toes in his excitement, "*That* is some crazy scary awesomeness!"

"What are you looking at?" Eva asked.

"This is a magical map of the course," Reese smiled. "I can't see the route until a contestant has already been there. This helps me figure out how far ahead the others are. If you're first, you still don't know the next obstacle."

"Does everyone get one of these?" Robert asked, trying to get a closer look.

"Only the people who've competed before."

"But you don't know how *many* people are ahead of you, right?" Eva asked.

"Right – only that at least one contestant has gotten that far. They may not make it through the next obstacle, and it certainly doesn't mean they'll win, but they've at least made it through the first obstacle. Look," she pointed, "someone else has already made it across the river and is at an obstacle called the Whipping Willow Wall.... Wow."

"Doesn't it seem like the people who *aren't* first have the better advantage?" Robert asked.

"It seems that way, but it's not about who finishes first. It's about who finishes with the most Luck intact!" Reese said. "My people are fiercely proud, and super competitive, but we still rely too much on Luck and not on each other to get things done."

Robert grimaced and continued, "Well, how are we going to get past The Ugly Wonder over there?" They poked their heads out from behind the tree and quickly ducked back again when the Troll turned his head in their direction.

"Trolls aren't known to have the best eyesight," Reese whispered, "but they do have an incredibly keen sense of smell. If we could just disguise our scent, maybe we could jump across this spot in the river to get by him?" She pointed to a bend in the river on the map.

"Wait - I have an idea," Robert said. "Maybe some high-tech titanium floaty shoes could fly us over!"

"Unless you actually packed some 'high-tech titanium floaty shoes' for this race, that won't work, genius," Eva snorted. "We're not using all of our Luck on that."

Before Robert could make a snarky comeback, Reese grabbed his arm. "You guys, get back!"

Pulling the children farther behind the tree, Reese put a finger to her lips and pointed toward the bridge. When they peeked through the leaves, they saw the Leprechaun with the blue balloon – Reese's father. Squatting a safe distance from the bridge, they watched him gently blow a bit of Luck onto the balloon tied to his wrist. Very faintly the breeze carried his chant through the air to their ears: "Fly me gently, straight on course, fast and sure like a racehorse!" In one graceful movement the balloon began to lift him into the air.

"Now *that* is a good idea! No wonder he was so concerned about that silly balloon," Robert whispered. Reese smiled proudly.

Then the wind changed.

"No, Da! Use more Luck!" she cried leaping up from the bush. "Da! The wind!" She yelled louder, cupping her hands around her mouth, but he continued floating, unaware.

Only when the Troll poked his head out from under the bridge and sniffed the air did Reese's father look toward the sound of Reese's desperate shouts. By then it was too late. Delighted that he had been airmailed a little snack, the Troll gleefully plucked his treat from the sky, popping the balloon with his sharp nails and flipping the Leprechaun upside down so that he now dangled by one ankle, unable to reach any of his Golden Luck.

Savoring his first catch of this year's contestants, the Troll slowly lifted him up over his open mouth to take a nice bite, relishing the smell of the Leprechaun's fear.

9. Lucky Charm

Reese watched her father gesticulating wildly, no doubt trying to convince the Troll that he was tough and leathery - and would not make a good meal.

"What do we do? What do we do?" Robert jumped up and down. Eva knew that it would be best to stay calm, but in a situation like this she could understand the need for hopping.

"Distract him! We have to distract him," Eva said, raising her Golden arm.

"No! I'll wish Da slippery!" Reese shouted, readying her arm to blow some of the Luck Dust.

But Robert had already begun to run toward to river. He flapped his arms over his head, screaming unintelligible threats as he raced toward the Troll.

"What is he doing?!"

"Uh… Well, if anyone can distract a troll, it's Robert," Eva said, trying to sound confident. She hoped her smile didn't seem as nervous as it really was. "But we should probably go help him just in case. Come on!"

As the two ran, Reese shouted, "I wish he'd have just listened for a minute! Is he always this reckless?"

"Oh, yes!" Eva yelled back. "That's part of his 'charm,' if you could call it that!"

"Hah!" Reese snorted. "A Lucky charm! How fortunate for him!"

Robert's earsplitting race to the bridge was

fortunate for Reese's *father* because the Troll stopped playing with his dinner and turned to look at the frenzied critter running toward him with his arms and legs flailing in all directions.

"Huh?" the Troll's deep voice boomed as he watched Robert approach.

"I say!" Robert yelled, skidding to a halt. He was still panting from his run but he managed to yell loudly, "You aren't going to eat him are you? Because I caught him just moments ago and I was planning to eat him myself. He slipped away from me, the rascal!"

The Troll rumbled, sniffing at Robert, "Urgh! You not Leprechaun... You too little to eat this one." He held his snack closer as if to keep Robert from snatching it. "What you?"

"What you? Oh! What *me*! I'm a Troll. You don't know a fellow Troll when you meet him?" Robert rumble-squeaked back.

The giant, green monster came closer to Robert and bent down to sniff him. "You too little to be Troll. You don't smell like Troll," he said skeptically.

"I *am* a Troll," Robert insisted backing away ever so slightly. "This is what... uhhh... This is what happens when you eat Leprechauns with white hair like *that!*" Robert pointed at Reese's father still struggling in the Trolls hands.

"White hair snack make Troll tiny?" the Troll lifted the Leprechaun up for a closer inspection. "And smell bad?"

"Yes, yes... I was once bigger than you. Uhhh, and *way* more ferocious," Robert lied, inching closer to the Troll. "I really should give those things up. Terrible habit, really... But you know what they say, right? 'A Troll's gotta do what a Troll's gotta do.'" Robert laughed nervously. "They do say that, right?"

"What is he doing?" Eva panicked.

"Look, Eva!" Reese grinned. "He turned the Troll's back to us! I think I can get to Da if I can bounce high enough."

"Bounce? Bounce on what?" Eva whimpered.

"Stand back," Reese said. "I don't know what to expect here, but I read up on a simple Luck wish they used in the Early Days. It's called 'Ditto.' If this works, just follow me. I'm going to try to reach Da while the Troll is distracted." She held her hands to her mouth and blew a puff of Golden Dust across the river. Soon translucent bubbles of all sizes bobbed to the surface and floated to the river's edge.

With a small whoop, Reese ran toward the shoreline and quickly studied them. They seemed look like normal bubbles – some were smaller than others; some had flattened into very large disks and were very springy to the touch. She reached to push a small bubble from the shoreline, hoping it would grow, but instead it popped.

"What are those?" Eva whispered, keeping the Troll in sight.

"They're called Bumble Boats," Reese whispered back. "They *should* hold up in the acid river... But I need more large ones, and that one popped when I touched it."

"Here, let me try something," Eva offered. "Maybe it's like blowing out a wish on a birthday cake." She hurried over to a bubble, and with a hearty breath, blew it into the river.

Reese patted Eva on the back and whispered "See? Teamwork!" There, in front of her, the bubble had not only stayed anchored to the place it landed, but it had multiplied, creating other bubbles which also flattened, becoming firm and bouncy. She reached out and tapped the surface, and it wobbled but stayed secure.

"Brilliant!" she hooted. "They work in the *acid*! We can bounce on the bubbles to cross the river and save my father! Come on!"

The bubbles bobbed and shuddered, but they stayed in place. Reese jumped first, landing squarely on a large bubble and bouncing straight up into the air, soaring higher with each bounce. After she got the feel of it, she launched herself to the next bubble. There she bounced a few times before springing to the next. And then the next.

Reese could hear Robert talking with the Troll when she reached a bubble floating near the center of the bridge. She jumped with as much force as she had in her wobbly legs, and reached for her father's thrashing hands as the Troll absently dangled him over the edge while he talked.

"I don't suppose you know this, but I used to be the Troll heavyweight wrestling champion of all the bridges... in the *universe*," she heard Robert say. "Yeah, I used to eat, like, ten Leprechauns before each match. Then I'd lift boulders just to warm up. I do about three thousand reps. What about you?" Robert shouted up at the Troll as he stomped his way closer.

"You tiny," the Troll insisted, looking confused.

"I might be small, but I'm surprisingly strong," Robert replied flexing one arm.

Just then, the troll dropped the Leprechaun. "You want arm wrestle?" he asked, leaning down to place his elbow on the bridge rail and extending his massive green hand toward Robert.

Behind the kneeling Troll, Reese crashed into her father mid-air – she on the way up, and he on the way down. They collided with surprise, and tumbled down together clinging to each other. The large bubble bounced them up again and again into Robert's view over the bridge. Each time they sprung into sight, Robert bit his tongue in order not to laugh, since they continued to pop up at the craziest angles. One time Reese bounced, spread-eagle, clutching her father's foot. Next, her father was head first into Reese's armpit, grabbing her neck.

Eva winced. None of them stood a chance if she didn't act fast. Gingerly, she stepped out onto the nearest bumble boat in the boiling purple river, testing it. When it didn't burst, she bounced onto it like it was a trampoline, and there she built up enough momentum to spring toward where Reese and her father were caught in an awkward bounce, unable to steady themselves.

When Robert saw Eva bouncing in and out of his view behind the Troll it became even more difficult to keep the Troll's attention, and more than once the Troll looked as if he was on the verge of ending their little conversation with one swift chomp. Robert gulped. This was not going well.

Eva heard snippets of Robert's scam while she jumped harder, getting her rhythm. Phrases like, "generally very popular amongst the lady Trolls..." and "usually do my workout routine before I eat too many..." and "in my off season I don't normally arm wres..." made it clear she'd better get Robert out of there – and fast!

But no one was more surprised than Eva herself when she shut her eyes and bounced her mightiest bounce, crashing into both Reese and her father in a mid- air tackle, knocking the wind out of them and hurtling all three across the river onto the shore of the other side. The three of them "oofed" and rolled and "umphed," stopping a safe distance from the acid water, desperately hoping the Troll hadn't heard any of it.

Robert's nose may not have been as keen as the Troll's but he could definitely see that his friends were no longer leaping into the air. "Welp... You know I *would* love a good old-fashioned arm wrestle with you, but I'm going to find another Leprechaun – one *without* white hair. I've eaten my share of those today, and I can't afford to get any smaller..." He had casually sauntered across the bridge until he was almost to the other side as he talked to the Troll. "You keep that one. You can afford to lose a few inches."

"Not lose inches. You take," the Troll said turning around to look for the Leprechaun.

As he turned his back, Robert pivoted and ran as fast as he could toward the opposite shore.

Noticing his snack was now gone, the Troll turned back to find the tiny, pale 'Troll' sprinting away. Roaring, he stretched his arms wide and splashed the roiling acid around him. He had been tricked! "Not small Troll!" he bellowed, making a quick grab for Robert as he leapt off the last part of the bridge. "Lying Leprechaun!"

"Robert! Run faster!" Eva shrieked.

"Run t' the tree line! Ye'll be safe thar!" Reese's father shouted, gripping his daughter's hand so tightly she feared her bones were going to crumble.

Leprechauns on the other side of the river, who had been plotting their course, now stood still and began to watch with excitement. The furious Troll thundered and roared, splashing river water with his angry fists, causing the cheering spectators to scatter.

"Uh oh…" Reese covered her mouth, her eyes growing wider. Drops of acid splattered the nearby trees, smoking leaves from their limbs. The smell of scorched grass clouded the air and birds began to take flight. Suddenly everything went silent. "He's coming out of the water!" Reese cried. "Da! Let's move it!"

Eva grabbed her pack tightly and followed the scattering Leprechauns toward the trees. "I thought trolls stayed under bridges!" she shouted as they dodged other contestants on the run.

"They can only chase us a short distance from their bridge. It's Troll Code!" Reese shouted back. "Now, head for the hills!"

Heavy footsteps and labored breath behind them caused Eva to sneak a peek over her shoulder. "Geesh, Robert!" Eva gasped as he caught up, "You really ticked him off." But Robert could simply nod, panting and clutching his heavy backpack.

They could now only focus on running as fast as their feet would carry them into the woods while the Troll crashed behind them, close enough to smell their fear.

10. Mushy-Mushy Talk

"Oh, Da," Reese panted, lying on the grass next to her father. "All your Golden Dust is gone."

They had continued running through the woods as long as they could, even after the Troll had finally stopped chasing them. Just as Robert and Eva were planning to abandon their packs, the Troll was yanked to a halt as if he was tied to a long tether that had finally reached its end. He boomed his disappointment and pounded the invisible barrier he could not cross. But even as they saw him roaring in the distance, their fear kept them running until they could no longer catch their breath and were forced to drop down onto the grass, gasping. It was then that Reese had noticed her father no longer wore *any* of the Golden Luck Dust he had carefully collected for so long.

"I had t' use it all t' make sure we reached the other side of the shore when yer friend here tackled us," he said wearily. "We couldn't've made it over the acid river without some Luck."

"Oh, Da! *Some* Luck. Not *all* of it!"

"More bodies t' take care of means more Luck needed t' take care of 'em," he shrugged. "What's a father t' do?"

She hugged him until he turned quite red with the show of affection. "Thank you, Da! That's the kind of help all Leprechauns should offer with their Luck. But what'll you do now?"

"Oh, I s'pose the same thing I've done every

other day: I'll head home and start savin' my Luck fer the next Tournament. Yer Mum was expectin' me fer supper t'night anyhow." He stood up and brushed off his britches. "I don't know about this 'shared effort' idea of yer's but I'm proud of ye. Don't ferget, darlin' – use yer cheapest wishes and save what ye can of yer Luck. Ye can win this year! Lordy knows ye were given plenty of smarts from yer family!" Then he winked at her and began to whistle as he walked away.

Reese giggled. "I get my smarts from Mum's side!" she called out. But her father kept walking and whistling, only waving back at them to show he had heard the joke.

The children watched him walk until he disappeared into the woods, and Eva became somber. "Reese, you've used some of your Luck to help us too," she said, looking at her friend who now wore Gold Dust from only the waist down. "Please! Save your Luck so you have enough to get a Coin at the end of the Tournament!"

"That's okay. I helped you because you're my friends, and it was the right thing to do. But I did it for my Da too. He's *got* to know that we're better when we work together. Besides, you helped us to the other side of the river. And Robert's crazy stories stopped the Troll from eating Da. I should be thanking *you.*"

They grinned at one another.

"Gah! Mushy-mushy talk," Robert interrupted, standing up and hoisting his backpack onto his back. "We get it! We're friends! Can we get going now? We've got a race to win and a friend to save." Eva and Reese groaned as they stood up and joined him, walking toward the flagged path marked for the Tournament.

"What's the next obstacle, Reese?" Robert asked, scrambling up the stone steps ahead of the girls. They were out of breath again climbing the trail up the steep dirt hill.

"Let me look at the map. Other contestants have surely made it this far already."

"Wait a minute…" Eva stopped dead in her tracks, causing the others to run into her.

"Whoah, a little warning next time?"

Eva stood nose to nose with Reese, scrutinizing her. "The Tournament is only held once every ten years, right? I thought you said you were ten!"

Just then Robert turned to look at Reese curiously. "You were only a *year old* when you competed in the last contest?"

"No, I said I was ten in The Land of Luck. In *your* world that makes me exactly one hundred years old."

Robert landed with a solid thud onto his back pack. "Geesh, you're ancient!"

"Robert! Rude!" Eva prodded him with her foot.

"What – my grandmother isn't even *that* old," he said staring harder at Reese.

"How come you look our age?"

Reese burst into laughter. "Actually, calling someone 'ancient' here is a great compliment! Thank you!" she giggled. "Come on; let's get to the top of the hill. I still can't see the next obstacle on the map, but maybe we can see it from there."

The girls went on ahead as Robert gathered up his pack and brushed off. The afternoon had become warm and they paused often to help each other over the large boulders and stumps along the inclined trail. They traded turns carrying Robert's pack, and even he seemed to question whether it had been wise to bring the basketball pump and hammer along. His cheerful quip, "You just never know" turned into a grumpy, "Are we almost there yet?" just as they finally reached the summit.

"I'm not really sure where 'there' is," Reese faltered. "But we're at what looks like the highest point of the trail..." They were out of breath and ready for a break, and Eva was beginning to think maybe one of the Leprechaun tricksters had sabotaged them by flagging the wrong trail or giving them a trick map.

Robert pulled off his backpack to get some water, and Eva sat down on a fallen tree stump to rummage around for her Junior Detective journal. Only Reese was unable to relax. As tired as she was, she felt responsible to guide their path (this was her Land after all) and she couldn't be sure what an ex-Tooth Fairy would do to their kidnapped friend if they didn't win the Golden Coin.

She wandered to the rim of the steep drop-off and scanned the terrain below. "That is so *weird*," she mused. "Hey, you two, come take a look at this. There's a house over that hill that looks just like an upside down tooth. It's like a big molar with all the pointy roots up in the air. I've never seen anything like it before."

Eva and Robert looked up, startled. "*What* did you just say?" Eva asked. Leaving their packs where they were as they hurried to Reese's side. There, in a clearing between two

hills was a large stone house.

"Why didn't any of the other contestants see this? It's like it was camouflaged or something... and what is that on the roof? Is it a filling?" Reese wondered aloud, unaware that her friends had grown pale.

"Actually," Eva almost whispered, "we saw something just like it in Fairy Land."

Robert nodded at her. "That must be where Diva lives now! Why would she choose *another* tooth house? She isn't even a Tooth Fairy anymore!"

"Wait. Wait. Wait!" Reese narrowed her eyes. "You're telling me the Tooth Fairy you told me about lives there? The one who steals candy and kidnapped your friend?"

"That is what I am telling you," Robert said.

"So, she just *flies* out of Fairy Land and *somehow* just *happens* upon another house shaped like a tooth in the Land of Luck?"

"She probably used some awful rotting helpers to build it," Eva said more to Robert than Reese. "She had some magic when she left so she probably used it to set up a house here... And it makes perfect sense when you think about it. She told us we'd meet up with her in the 'The Land of Luck.' That must be her house." She hopped up and down, "And if that's her house, that's where Lauren is!"

"Brilliant deduction, *detective*," Robert smirked.

Eva gave him the stink-eye and turned her back on him to talk with Reese. "We need to rescue Lauren."

"I thought you two were going to win a Gold Coin so you could *wish* her back home."

"We can't take a chance. We may not have enough Golden Luck at the end of the contest to win a Coin. I think we should use what we have *now* to save her while we're here," Eva explained. "I'm sorry, Reese, but we can't leave Lauren now that we're this close. You'll have to finish the Tournament without us." Robert nodded and reached out to pat her on the shoulder.

Reese looked back and forth between her two new friends. "I'm coming along," she grinned. "If that's okay, I mean."

"You can't! What about the Tournament?

You can become a Leader of the Land like your father said. You can do it!" Robert insisted.

"My message to the Leprechauns is more important than winning the Tournament! My people need to see the importance of friendship and how working together can accomplish... well... *anything!*" Reese smiled. "Besides, I've never really had friends before."

They looked at each other in silence for a moment before Eva grinned, "Well then, I guess it's decided. I say we sneak in. The element of surprise is our best option."

"All for one..." Robert whispered.

Reese responded, "And one Lucky chance!"

11. I'm Rubber, You're Glue

The children crept along the dense, untamed path down the side of the hill, staying close to the trees and bushes as they made their way silently toward the stone house. Every snapped twig and fluttering leaf made them hold their breath, hoping they hadn't set off any alarms the ex-Tooth Fairy may have installed around her new fortress. The fact that the upside down tooth did not appear to have any windows eased their anxiety, but not by much.

"I don't see any guards," Eva whispered,

scanning the roofline. "But that doesn't mean she doesn't have any."

Robert sighed, "What would they do anyway? Floss us to death? Let's just go." Then without warning, he was scampering through the grass away from them.

"Seriously?" Reese whispered. "How has he made it to age nine?"

Eva grabbed Reese's hand and sprinted after Robert, vowing to herself that she was going to reevaluate his status in their Junior Detective Club if they made it out of this alive.

When the girls slumped against the tooth, panting, Robert was already busy examining the home. "No wonder Diva doesn't think she needs a guard," he said, running his hand back and forth across the smooth stone and looking up at the roof. "How do you get into this place? We can't climb this – and the roof is so far up there!"

Eva and Reese were still trying to catch their

breath, when Reese pointed upward, shielding her eyes from the sun. "I think I see a crack at the top," she said.

"And are those fans on the roots? Why would fans pull *in* dust?" Eva asked squinting at the odd sight.

"Those fans aren't drawing in any ordinary dust!" Reese gasped. "That's our Luck! That must be why we're having the shortage! She's been drawing it all *here*."

The children stood studying the fans. They seemed to create a vacuum that drew the air in and filtered out the Gold Dust particles.

"I wonder how the fans attract the Gold in the first place," Eva mused.

"Yeah," Robert said. "And why wouldn't she have guards up there?"

"Maybe she does," Reese gulped.

A shiver of fear ran through Eva as she remembered the last guards Diva had hired for her tooth home – the disgusting Rot

Guards. "We need to figure out some way to get inside and find Lauren. There aren't any windows, and we certainly can't just knock on the front door and ask if we can use her bathroom."

They each sat on the ground, thinking. At last Reese said, "This is a bit of a long shot, but we *could* try the Rubber-Glue wish. It doesn't use much Luck – which is good – but it'll only work with two people."

"Uh... You lost me," Eva looked puzzled.

"Do you know the rhyme 'I'm rubber, you're glue – what you say bounces off me and sticks to you?'"

"Do I know it!" Robert laughed. "I've perfected it!"

Reese continued, "I discovered with some classmates when I was little that if you say that rhyme and follow it by blowing Golden Luck dust, one person becomes super sticky and the other person gets super rubbery!" Reese laughed. "It's hilarious! But it only lasts for a minute. Maybe if we used it the sticky person could climb to the top."

"Like Spiderman? Count me in!" Robert shouted, hopping up and down.

"My goodness! Your world has men that are spiders? Ugh!" Reese clutched her stomach.

"No, no – there's only one Spiderman and his is definitely not ugh. He's *cool!*" Robert reassured her.

"What about the rubbery person?" Eva asked.

"The rubbery person can stretch a bit but I don't think you could reach to the roof."

"I brought some dental floss," he volunteered. "We could help the last person up with that."

"Perfect! I'll stay down here and you two can do the climb," Eva decided.

"Okay," he said. "How do we do this?"

"You say the rhyme. Then you make the wish," she said. "But when you do, remember to not to blow too hard. The Luck

Dust only comes off if you're gentle. Like blowing out a candle."

"Got it," Robert nodded. "Here goes nothing..." He quickly recited the rhyme and squeezed his eyes shut. When he gently blew on the palm of his hand, the Golden Dust swirled into the air, then settled on him for just a moment before it bounced off and flew toward Reese in a fine mist. When it landed, the glittery Luck latched on to her sticky limbs firmly, and she wasted no time, quickly leaping forward to begin the climb. Getting her bearings for a brief second, she stood on the side of the house and looked up. *It isn't that far away*, she reasoned with herself.

Robert began to bob up and down. "Come! On! Reese! You! Can! Do! This!" He shouted each word of encouragement as his limbs bounced and wobbled like gelatin.

Reese nodded at them, and with a deep breath she began her ascent, slowly at first, just to get the feel of it. It had been awhile since she'd used this wish, and now wasn't the time to botch it. When she looked back, she saw Eva mouth the words *go faster*, so she picked up her pace, jogging up the wall as if she was running on flat ground, each footstep making a sticky sucking sound.

In no time she was at the top. She gripped the edge and disappeared over the side as the children stared and silently cheered her success from below.

"Whew!" Eva said. "One down."

"You! Mean! One! Up!" Robert countered.

Reese's head popped back over the side and she called down softly, "Okay! Now, Eva, you say the rhyme to Robert. It's his turn to get sticky!" She laughed. "Robert, stop bouncing! And when you're sticky, remember that you have to hurry!"

Eva tapped him impatiently. "You ready?" Robert nodded glumly and she said, "Okay... 'I'm rubber, you're glue. What I say bounces off me and sticks to you!'" She made her wish and blew gently. Again, the Dust rose in a cloud and bounced from her palms to stick to Robert.

Immediately his bouncing stopped and he laughed with glee, placing his hands on the home's smooth surface. "This is so *weird!*" he giggled, crawling toward Reese. "Eva, you gotta try this." He shuffled up the wall and turned to look down at her. "Do I look like Spiderman?"

Eva struggled to stand up straight on her now wobbly legs. "No," she said. "You look like a crazy boy. And remember – you have to hurry!"

"What about now?" He scurried in a circle, pretending to shoot a web from his wrist. "Fear not! I'll save you, *for I am Robertman!*"

Eva felt like she was back on one of the bubbles on the acid river, and tried to keep as still as possible.

"This is even more fun than being rubbery!" He sounded giddy.

But almost as soon as it had started, the

children's spell began to dissipate. Feeling her limbs becoming more solid, Eva shouted, "Robert! It's starting to wear off! Move it!"

"What? Did you say 'boing, boing, boing'?" he laughed, scampering up the side of the wall. "Hey! You should see this!" he shouted, pointing into the distance. "You can see everything from here!"

"Robert!" Reese called. But it was already too late. Robert had begun to slide.

"What should I do!" he shouted up at Reese.

"Use your luck!" she shouted back urgently.

Robert clumsily got his feet under him and gingerly let go of the building so he could bring his hands up to his mouth - just as the spell of the rhyme evaporated completely. "Heeeellp!" he shrieked as the suction released, and he fell back toward the ground where Eva watched in horror.

"Robert!" Eva called out. She raised her hands to her mouth, praying for a safety net, before blowing a double dose of her Luck up

toward him.

The Dust swirled, and Eva watched in amazement as the Golden glitter seemed to form a huge open hand catching Robert in its palm. The hand cushioned him, then lowered and released him near the ground, rolling him through the grass where he stopped at Eva's feet.

"Oh, Eva! *Thank* you for catching me!" he breathed shakily.

"I didn't catch you," she said, looking at her arms and legs, which were now back to their normal color. Only a tiny bit of Gold remained on the tips of her shoes.

"Your Luck..." Robert looked sheepish. "It's almost all gone... because I was fooling around..."

"Well, it had to be done... I guess I'll just have to be careful with the little bit I have left. Maybe I can still win a penny's worth of Luck," she grinned at Robert. "Get it? A Lucky penny?"

Robert grinned back at her and stood up. "Thanks again for saving me." He shuffled his feet and punched her shoulder lightly.

"I'm sure it won't be the last time," she scowled, and punched him back (a little harder).

"How are we going to get to the roof without using the rest of your Luck?" he looked concerned.

Reese called down, "You guys don't need to worry about how much Luck you have left. Use it all and get up here. You will not *believe* this!"

12. Just My Luck

"You might as well just use all of the Luck and wish us up there," Eva sighed. "It sounds like we don't have to ration it now..."

"Sure," Robert shrugged. He lifted his palms, took a huge breath and blew. Eva watched as all of the Golden Luck drained from him like water being poured from a bottle. It gathered in front of the children like a Golden box and Eva giggled when an elevator door opened and Robert gestured to her saying, "After you madam," like he was some kind of grand gentleman.

When the doors opened again they were safely at the top without a single speck of Luck Dust left on either of them. There they found Reese intently examining the cause of Leprechaun Land's Luck shortage.

"Cool!" Robert shouted. But Reese's face was clouded with anger. On top of the tooth, looking for all the world like a huge filling, was a deep golden pool. The fans they had seen from the ground were drawing the Golden dust from the sky and depositing it into the pool in trickles.

"Well this brings a whole new meaning to the saying 'just my Luck,'" Robert scoffed. "Apparently *everyone's* Luck is Diva's Luck!"

"We can't leave it this way!" Reese said, the tips of her ears growing red with anger. "This evil Diva did not *earn* the Luck! She's stealing it. This could destroy Leprechaun society. We have to do something!"

"Of course. But we have to save Lauren too," Eva reminded her.

"I have an idea." Robert slung his backpack from his shoulders and rooted around until he had produced a small hammer, some nails and a water bottle.

"Of course, he brought a hammer and nails..." Eva muttered to herself. "What can't a hammer or some candy fix?" She shook her head, thinking she should write down a list of "standard" adventure tools in her Jr. Detective notebook so they didn't lug around unnecessary weight all the time.

"Reese saw a crack in the tooth over here, remember?" he said. "Maybe we can make the crack bigger and drain the Luck from the pool." He walked over to the edge of the tooth roof and ran his fingers along the crack. "Is this what you saw?" Reese nodded.

Robert gently hammered a nail into the gap causing it to fracture and split. When the crack stopped, he moved to its end and hammered the next nail, each time moving closer to the Golden pool. In time he had hammered ten nails along the split, like he was laying rail road tracks, and now the crack reached from the edge of the roof all the way to the edge of the pool. Reese held her breath as Robert hammered away at the edge of the pool until they saw the Golden liquid Luck begin to seep its way into the crevice and flow along the broken tooth until it reached the edge. Once at the edge, it seeped down the side of the tooth home in a Golden stream, while some of it scattered back into the wind.

"That should do it," Robert said leaning over the edge and watching the crack begin to extend down the side. He stood up and turned to his friends with a grin, "Let's take a quick dip before it's all gone. Last one in is a rotten tooth!"

"I don't know..." Reese hesitated. "This is stolen Luck."

Eva took her hand, "We'll need some to save Lauren. I thought this is what you meant when you suggested your people share Luck for a greater purpose."

Reese looked back at her and squeezed her

hand with a nod. "Yes. To save Lauren." Then they ran after Robert holding hands and laughing.

At the edge of the Luck pool they paused and Reese shouted, "For Lauren!" She pinched her nose and leaped from the side, cannon-balling with such a splash that Robert had to wipe the Golden 'liquid' from his hair.

He looked at Eva and said, "Ready? One... Two... Thrrr..." But before he could finish, Eva had already pushed him in.

"Three!" she shouted, and jumped in after him.

Under different circumstances, and if they'd had more time, the children would have spent time playing. But there was a Tournament to win, and Lauren to rescue, and so their swimming had to end.

When they emerged, they were again covered head to toe in Gold that dried on them in sticky Golden sparkles. "And now a little something in case we run into some guards,"

Robert said, leaning down and filling up the empty water bottle he had pulled from his pack.

"We're going to need to disable the fans," Reese said. "Otherwise, they'll just keep sucking the Luck back here."

"How do we do that?" Robert asked. "Can't we just *wish* the fans to stop working?"

"We've used Luck in some pretty big ways and you saw how quickly it's lost," Reese replied. "I think you have the wrong idea about it. Wishing and Luck can help, but they shouldn't replace good engineering and solid work. It's like my Da always used to say: 'Don't go wastin' yer wishes when ye can use yer noggin.' If we wished for everything, we'd end up tripping over bikes and toys and money everywhere. It would ruin our economy."

The children stared at her. It was exactly the same thing they'd heard about wishes in Fairy Land.

Reese walked over to each of the fans, ripping out the cords as she went, causing the wires to split and fray. Then she turned and grinned at them, holding up the ruined wires. "There. *That* was some solid work. Now, let's go find your friend. I saw a door by one of the fan sockets. Over here."

The friends moved from the quickly-emptying pool in search of their way down from the roof. "This must be what Diva uses to access the roof when she needs Luck," Eva said when they stood in front of a heavy stone door.

"Wait! Don't open it yet," Reese said, reaching into her pocket and pulling out a large leaf. "This is a Lily Fern Fumble," she told them. "I can hear what's on the other side of doors and walls with this." She rolled the leaf into a tube which she held to her ear, listening intently for any sounds inside. "It's quiet. I think we're safe," she said reaching for the handle.

"It's not locked!" Eva said in amazement as

she watched Reese turn the knob easily.

"Well, go on," Robert urged. "That crack is getting bigger by the second!"

Reese nodded and pushed her shoulder to the door when it was suddenly yanked open from the other side. The children gasped in horror as they now stood face to face with a lumpy, yellow and brown man clothed in a filthy military-looking uniform.

Or... they *would* have been face to face had the man been given a face. He seemed to be sculpted of clay with the necessary arms and legs, but the sculptor forgot to give the man any markings of eyelids or lips. He didn't appear to even have much of a nose. The two blobs that passed as ears stood away from the larger blob of his head and the neck that supported it seemed to mold right into the uniform he wore.

Reese screamed as he stepped forward and effortlessly picked her up.

Robert launched himself at the man, kicking him in the shins, but he left only the soft imprint of his shoe on the clay man's leg. "Yuck! What *are* you?" he cried, sticking out his tongue in disgust. Jumping to the side to avoid the man's reach, he stumbled into a second uniformed clay man who had come through the doorway and grabbed Robert from behind. Before Robert could clamp his mouth shut, his outstretched tongue licked his captor's arm and he gagged, "Ear wax! I'm gonna hurl! These guys are made of ear wax!"

Reese screamed louder, trying to bring her hands near her mouth to make a wish, but the wax man held her arms firmly at her side while another pounced on Eva.

It was a quick ambush, and each guard was mindful to hold the children with their arms down so they were unable to make a wish. "Mmm... Stopp strugggling," the first waxman said from the slit in its blank, lumpy face. Its voice sounded deep and heavy. "Divvva is waiting for you bbelow."

"Uchh, your breath is disgusting," Eva said turning her head away.

"Put me down!" Reese shouted kicking back at her captor's legs with all her strength.

But their screams and struggles didn't affect the guards at all. In fact, they didn't seem to notice much of anything on their own. They methodically carried the wiggling children into a narrow, grey hall that looked as though it was made of polished granite, down one stairwell and through several chambers until, after a dizzying number of turns, they finally descended a grand curved stairwell and reached the ground floor.

Another wax man met them there and led them across a black and white tiled entry. Turning to the others, he droned, "Pput them in the livving roomm with the other onne." He opened a set of ornate double doors and ushered the guards inside, where they simultaneously released the children onto the shiny floor.

After an unceremonious kick, the guards turned to leave while the children slipped and skidded their way to the far side of the room, only stopping once they had tumbled against the distant wall in a heap. Then the door slammed shut with a 'bang' that echoed in the hard, cold room.

In the silence, Robert groaned trying to sit up. "Well, what now?"

Eva felt a hand on her shoulder, and while she should have felt cheered that none of them were hurt, she just wanted to lie on the floor and feel sorry for herself for a while. It seemed nothing was going right.

"Eva? Is that you? Robert? You guys are all Golden! What in the world did you fall in this time?"

Eva opened her eyes and stared into the green eyes of her best friend. "Lauren!" Eva cried reaching up and hugging her. "We found you!"

Lauren tried to hug Eva back but she slipped and fell on top of her instead.

"Sorry," Lauren laughed. "The wax guards make everything around here so slippery!"

"Are you okay?" Robert asked reaching out to steady her.

"I'm fine. I thought maybe she was trying to bore me death! She just has me sitting here all day. No TV. No books. Hmph! It's dreadful, I tell you!"

Eva hugged her tighter. "Well, we're getting out of here now, and believe me – you won't need TV when I tell you the story of how we got here." She pointed at Reese, who was trying to right her hat. "That's Reese," she said. Reese gave her a grin. "She is an actual *real* Leprechaun!"

"And I outwitted a troll!" Robert said, jumping up and catching himself before he slipped to the ground again. Undeterred, he continued, "And Reese is actually one *hundred* years old. And there's a pool at the top of this house filled with Gold! And can you believe Diva actually chose another tooth house to live in – even though she's not even a real Tooth Fairy anymore?"

Lauren blinked back and forth at her friends.

Reese laughed, "I know. There's a lot to share... but seriously," she continued, "who lives in a tooth made of polished stone and uses disgusting ear wax as guards?"

"I do, my dear," snarled a voice at the doorway.

13. Great Cleaners But No Brains

Diva stood in the doorway sneering at the jumble of children across the room. She wore a fancy evening dress that glinted with familiar Golden Luck Dust as she walked. Her gown was snug around the top of her slightly plump figure. It appeared she'd stepped into the Luck pool deep enough to reach the bodice of her dress because the Gold stopped there and she looked as though she wore elbow-length Golden gloves. Her white hair was piled high and she had adorned it with a large Golden tiara that looked very much like a crown. As usual, she wore a great deal of makeup, but Eva noticed that Diva had one obvious change: The fairy wings that had been on her back when they saw her last were now gone.

"I'm delighted you accepted my invitation for a swap," Diva drawled, glaring at the children as she stepped into the room with wax guards following her. They lurched with squishy, squeaky steps until they blocked the door and surrounded the children. "And I see you brought an uninvited guest... I guess I shouldn't be surprised at your manners considering the way you acted in my home the last time we met."

"Why would you use ear wax guards in a polished stone home, uh tooth... *Whatever* this place is!" Reese asked, standing up (then slipping, and sitting back down).

"It makes perfect sense, stupid girl!" Diva chided her. "They polish the place simply by walking around. I mean, I get house cleaners *and* guards all in one! It's a *bargain*."

"Where do you find such disgusting household help? First the Rot Guards and now them?" Robert pointed at the ear wax men and attempted to stand up. "Do you know I accidently *licked* one?"

"Serves you right!" Diva cackled. "But to answer your question, it *is* very hard for decaying and rotten things to find work. I'm one of the few who advertises for their help. Like I said, it's a bargain. Humans are so thoughtless! You create them and then just throw them away and there they remain – in Nowhere Land – until someone is able to find use for them."

"Lady, I don't think you should be talking about *our* manners!" yelled Eva, who could not stand it anymore. "*You* kidnapped our friend!" She stood up and braced herself, awkwardly skating forward on the waxy floor, pointing a finger at Diva.

"Ohh... Cool," Robert whispered, looking at Lauren and Reese to make sure they noticed Eva's slide as well. The girls nodded quietly back at his silent message and smiled.

"I should think my note explained all of that," Diva hissed. "You owe me some baby teeth! After all, it was your idea to *give* them to me and now look. I've had to move out of my beautifully remodeled tooth home in elegant Fairy Land to the back woods of Leprechaun Land!" She threw up her hands and gestured around her, shaking her head.

Eva narrowed her eyes at Diva, giving her the stink eye. "We aren't going to give you anything! You stole the Halloween candy and you put us in your Decaying Dungeon!"

"Yes, well... I won't make that mistake again!" Diva said. "I'll take your baby teeth now, thank you!" She raised her palms and blew a steady stream of Golden Luck into the room until only the tips of her shoes remained gold.

The cloud lassoed Reese first, and she was instantly wrapped from neck to toe in golden chains. "Run!" she shouted, struggling against the restraints. Eva was roped next, and she fell hard onto the floor as the chains bound her legs and arms tightly.

Robert, who was on a junior hockey team, and Lauren, who had taken figure skating lessons for years, didn't need to think twice before pushing off from where they were standing, gliding quickly in the opposite direction from the cloud. They skated across the slippery floor like professionals.

"Get those little brats!" Diva commanded.

At once, the wax guards lumbered after the children, but their path of attack moved them directly into the Golden cloud, and the spell Diva had created to capture the children wrapped Golden chains around their pliable limbs instead, toppling several of them to the floor.

"Ah! You idiots!" Diva huffed, crossing her arms. "You used up my wish." The puff of Luck Diva had blown was, in fact, now gone, depleted by the guards who had run into it. "Great cleaners, but no brains..." she mumbled to herself, looking at her gown and arms which now revealed their original colors. "Such a pity... This Dust is gone so quickly."

"Of course it's gone quickly," Reese said with disgust, hopping around in her chains. "It's the magic of Luck – it's not unlimited wishes! You are greedy and evil."

Diva came closer, pointing a sharp nail at Reese's nose. "And *that* is why I will have your baby teeth! The unlimited magic from your teeth will allow me to...." She paused and took a closer look at Reese's ears. "Well, well..." she sneered. "I see we have a Leprechaun among us! What a treat!" She clapped her hands, delighted. "It's always a special thrill when a Leprechaun gets caught up in its own device."

"Luck isn't a 'device,'" Reese scowled. "And I hardly think I deserve to be called an 'it.' I do have feelings, you know."

"Well, no matter," Diva continued as if she hadn't heard Reese. "I have plenty more Luck where that came from. And you, my dear, should learn not to *push your Luck* with that mouth of yours." Diva brought up her hand and gently blew the last of the Luck from her shoes at Reese which pushed her off her feet and rolled her along the floor.

She laughed as Reese bumped and bumbled in her Golden chains. "*Push* your Luck! *Push!* Honestly, I am too clever," she said, dabbing at her heavily made up eyes. Then she turned and called toward Lauren and Robert, "Where could you two possibly go?" Diva nearly hopped up and down with glee, watching them skate to the farthest corner of the room.

The guards stood numbly in front of the only doors. "There's no other way out," she sung to them. "Do you see any windows? No, I didn't think so. Now, be little darlings, won't you, while I step upstairs for a just moment to get a little more Golden Luck? I promise I'll be riiight back." She held her skirt and walked carefully toward the door. "Yes... *Right* back to pull all those lovely baby teeth right out of your heads!"

Diva pointed at the nearest wax guard and said, "You there! Unchain your wax co-workers. And you! Watch this door!" She slammed the door behind her.

"We have to hurry," Robert whispered, skating closer to Lauren. "She is *not* going to be happy when she discovers what's happened to her pool."

"What do you mean?" Lauren asked.

"Look," Robert said pointing to the crack that had begun working its way down the side of a wall, "That's a crack we started on the roof!"

"Oh, my…" Lauren gasped. "It's all the way down here now? Do you know how tall this house is? It could break in half at any moment!"

Just then, they heard a faint screech bellowing all the way above them from the roof, "EEEAAAHH! HOW DARE YOU! I WILL DESTROY YOU ALL!"

"Wow, if we can hear Diva in *this* room, I think we have even bigger problems…" he winced. "We started the crack at the Luck pool. If it's all the way down here, the pool must be drained completely by now."

"Robert!" Reese shouted at him, "Maybe we could talk more about this later? Hurry up and use your Luck to free us!"

"All of it?" he whined. He glanced over at the wax guards but they seemed focused only on the last instructions given to them. Four stood firmly in front of the doors and one fixated on detangling the others from their chains.

"Robert!" Eva shouted. "Just use it and get us out of here!"

Lauren glided over to the struggling girls and pushed them toward each other so they could sit up. Robert closed his eyes for a moment and blew a mighty stream of Luck toward them, and when the Dust settled, their chains had dissolved into a droopy, sticky mass where it melted onto the ground. "Okay," he cried to his friends, "Follow me!"

Lauren helped Eva and Reese get to their feet, bringing up the rear and steadying Eva when she threatened to bring Reese down with her. Robert led the way, gliding slowly, unconcerned that the guards might stop them. He guided them toward the cracked wall and stopped them just in front. Turning to the girls and giving them a confident nod, he raised his palm and blew an expansive puff of Luck onto the wall's surface. Looking sheepish he said, "What? So I kept a little back."

His Golden Luck painted the wall thickly and the children watched for any sign of its collapse. Robert had used up all of his Luck, and now stood expectantly, hoping he hadn't made a big mistake.

Reese held herself at the ready, in case they needed some luck... like maybe suddenly finding a solid umbrella to shield them from falling granite.

Silence.

"What exactly did you wish?" Eva

wisecracked. "Because if it was for 'three of my friends to stare at a Golden wall' then you are brilliant."

Robert shook his head. "I don't understand," he said. "I wished for the wall to open up so we could get out."

"I keep telling you, Luck isn't like wishes," Reese said. "*Sometimes* you have to put a little work into it. Sometimes the harder you work the Luckier you get." She winked, bringing her fist to the wall and giving it a little knock.

They glanced nervously toward the guards again, but the wax men were still focused on Diva's last command, ignoring them altogether. The children shrugged at each other and continued to watch the wall. A large crack appeared, spreading more quickly with each knock, crackling and splitting into two veins in a large "V."

The house groaned and shuddered, and now they began to pound the stone in the center of the two cracks until, finally, each crack met the ground in a rumble. The stone in the middle crumbled and fell away, opening up a large triangular door to the outside.

"Nice Job, Hero!" Reese grinned.

Robert blushed and grinned back.

"Freedom!" Lauren squealed, clapping her hands, and missing the reference to Robert's new middle name.

"Now, come on!" Eva shouted. "We better get going before…"

The doors to the room flew open, knocking the wax men into a heap. "Before what?" Diva said, stalking into the shuddering room with her fists clenched at her sides.

14. The Domino Effect

Eva dove for the newly-made door and scrambled over the rubble of rocks with her friends right behind. They sprung to the ground outside the fallen wall and landed with a hard jolt.

"Oh, no! Our backpacks!" Robert cried.

Reese leapt up and shouted, "I'll go back for them. You stay here!"

"No, Reese, we can't let you go back in there alone!" Lauren wailed.

"I'll be fine," she said holding up her arms. "Look, I've still got all my Luck left. Diva's no match for me – we've drained her pool, remember?" She gave them the thumbs up and turned to Lauren. "Your friends have done some pretty heroic things to rescue you. I've never had friends like that before."

Lauren nodded, understanding what Reese was unable to explain: They were all in this together now. Friends for life – in Leprechaun years or human years – they would do anything to keep each other safe.

Reese patted Lauren's shoulder and mouthed *thank you*, before turning to scramble back up the cracked granite boulders, leaving the others holding hands and fretting.

"What are you doing??" Diva yelled at her wax guards, pointing behind her to the hole Reese now peeped through, just out of eyesight. "I told you not to let them escape!"

"You tollld us nottt to lettt themmm through thisss doorrr... Wwwe haven't," mumbled the guard in charge of the door.

"Sheee tolddd me to unnn-chain theeese guyyys..." said another. Reese strained to understand their gummy voices. It was the first time she'd heard them say more than a couple words, and she found them very hard to understand.

"IDIOTS! Do I have to spell out every little instruction? I want the children as my prisoners. *Prisoners!* Don't let them get away!"

"Ohhh... Of courrrse Mmmistress!" the wax guard burbled, and they all staggered into action, moving right past Reese, who had flattened her back against the wall in an effort to get out of their way.

"Why is it so hard to find good villain help these days?" Diva grumbled, shaking her head at the sight of more guards scattered around on the floor lying on top of one another with arms and legs everywhere. The house moaned again, and Diva yelped, gathering her skirt and tiptoeing carefully away from the hole in her wall.

"You there! On the ground! After those children!" she cried, backing toward the safety of the doorway, where the flying rubble had not yet begun to spread. (Of course, even Diva knew that in an earthquake, a doorway is the safest place to be!)

Reese knew she'd better get through the door to retrieve the backpacks before the guards started pouring through, or they'd clog the only entrance she now stood a chance of reaching. Diva was too distracted with the ruin of her home to notice that the children had left their very important belongings behind.

Distracted... Wait, Reese thought. *That gives me an idea.* As the wax guards began to reassemble themselves in more or less orderly fashion, Reese lifted her wrist and blew a gentle puff of Luck toward the back of the room. There, where Diva stood trembling (with anger or fear – or a combination of both – Reese couldn't tell) appeared a spectacularly glittering gem about the size of a large fist.

"Hello, what is this?" Diva said, noticing the glint. Stepping closer toward it with eager outstretched fingers, Diva fairly squealed with delight. "Oooh! What Luck! Maybe this little housequake isn't such a bad thing! It seems to have unearthed this charming..." Diva grunted as her fingers pried at the stone, "... beauty of an... *emerald!*" She sucked in her breath and nearly swooned as she pulled at the gem.

Reese crept into the room while she had her chance. Gliding awkwardly toward the backpacks, she extended her arms, this served to both steady herself and to help reach the supplies.

Diva had forgotten the wax men altogether, as she had now popped the gemstone out of its spot in the wall and was crooning over it as if it was her own infant. "Ooh, yes yes yes, my pretty little one. Who loves you, precious? Who loves you? Mommy loves you," she cooed in a baby voice that made Reese roll her eyes.

With Diva occupied, Reese silently snagged the backpacks and turned to cautiously skate toward the broken doorway. The guards had finally managed to untangle themselves and get into formation, and when they began marching toward Reese, she froze in terror.

However, they did not seem to even see her as they shuffled forward on their single-minded mission, and even though she was fully prepared to use additional Luck Dust, the guards merely parted and marched around her.

Shaking her head in confusion Reese, turned and skated for all she was worth. She still had a chance to make it through the doorway ahead of the guards. As she glided forward, she realized she was going to have to push through them in order to escape. Panting and slipping, she built up speed and pushed the wax man in front of her, running across his body when he fell, and bursting through the line of blob men. She popped through the hole in the wall clutching the backpacks and landed just in front of the mass of guards, who continued to ignore her as they began pouring out of the house like sap from a tree.

At the top of the wall, Reese jostled the backpacks and grabbed a couple of rocks. Careful not to disturb the pile of granite that was her way down, she stepped lightly, balancing the supplies and using her elbows to descend. "You guys!" she shouted over the side. The children's eyes were wide in horror as globs of wax seemed to be oozing arms and legs from the hole in the tooth.

"Catch these!" Reese set the rocks down and tossed the backpacks to them.

They grabbed their packs and began to scramble away as Reese turned and pelted the guards that had already begun to pass her. "Take that!" She threw the first rock and watched it sink into the back of a guard's wax body, causing him to lose his balance and fall into another. Soon other guards were tripping over the fallen brown blobs in a domino effect.

The children stopped to watch as Reese

launched another stone. It landed square in the middle of another guard's back, sticking there, and knocking him off his feet.

None of the guards turned to see where the source of this ambush was coming from, so Reese scooped up several more rocks. By now she was taking them out so quickly that the children decided to take a seat on the clover-filled lawn so they could watch and cheer her on. In fact, Reese, growing winded, decided to alter her plan of attack, and merely walked over to the line of guards snaking from the hole in the tooth and began tripping them.

They continued to ignore her, falling over each other in succession, while Reese clowned around for her cheer squad. "Whoopsie daisy!" she shouted, pushing the next guard that popped out of the entrance. The children laughed and clapped loudly as each guard toppled.

"Why aren't they capturing you?" Eva shouted as another brown blob landed in the heap.

"I just figured that out myself!" Reese shouted back. "Diva told them to go get the *children*. I'm a Leprechaun!" She jigged and bowed, sticking out her tongue at the next wax guard. "Watch this!" She stuck out her foot, and the wax man, who kept right on walking in his pursuit of the children, tumbled over mindlessly.

"I don't think she's going to let us go so easily! Leave the rest and run!" Lauren shouted as Diva, who had finally put down her precious gem, climbed out over the house wreckage.

"You horrible children! Look what you've done to my home! You will pay for this with your baby teeth!" She shook her fist at them. "I will *peel* the Luck you stole from me *off your bones!*"

Eva launched a sizeable stone at the wax guard standing next to Diva, causing him to stumble and fall backward into the screaming former Tooth Fairy, knocking them both over and giving Reese time to run and join the others.

"You idiot! Get off me and get them!" Diva screeched and slapped at the blob on top of her.

"Alll of themmm?"

"Of course! What did you think I meant?" she shrieked.

"That one iss a Leppprechaunnn. You sssaid it yourrrselfff."

"Oh, for crying out loud!" Diva pounded her fists against the ground. "Yes! Yes! Capture *all* of them!"

The children's eyes widened; they would no longer be able to play any tricks, as Diva had given very precise orders the sticky guards now understood. Quickly they oozed into formation and were now streaming forward in a dangerous battle line.

"How many do you think there are?" Robert shouted, hugging his backpack and leaping to his feet.

"Enough to completely absorb us in their goo!" Reese shouted. "Now run!"

The friends sped away, stumbling over mossy rocks and slippery grass.

"Where are we going?" Lauren puffed as they ran.

"We should try to get back to town. They wouldn't dare go there once the other Leprechauns know she's been stealing our Luck!" Reese huffed.

They struggled up the hill leading back to the marked Tournament trail. When Eva looked behind them and saw even more wax guards pouring out of the broken wall from below, an idea occurred to her.

"Wait, wait!" she panted when they were halfway up the slope. "Robert, give me the water bottle you filled with Luck."

"What are you going to do? You have plenty of your own Luck left," he gasped, stopping to slide his backpack off and retrieve the Golden water bottle.

"I'm just going to give us a little more time to escape," she grinned. She pulled off her backpack and pulled out a small Official Junior Detective Magnifying Glass. It was among her prized possessions, and she had spent long hours completing many Junior Detective questionnaires in order to win it. "Every good detective has a magnifying glass."

"We aren't looking for clues," Lauren wheezed, leaning on her knees to catch her breath. (Even though she didn't think running was very ladylike, based on their recent adventures, she was beginning to reconsider her stance on exercise.)

"I think we can melt the guards," Eva said with a grin. "The glass will magnify the heat of the sun and turn them to blobs! *Melted* blobs, I mean..."

"That's very evil genius of you, but it's just too small," Robert shook his head.

"I know... But with a little... well a *lot* of Luck," she shook the water bottle, "we can get more heat." Eva grinned at him and turned to face the wax guards. She leaned down, pushed the handle of the magnifying glass into the ground and stood back.

"Hurry, Eva! They're coming up the hill faster now," Reese urged.

Eva nodded and opened the Golden bottle. She tipped it toward the magnifier as if pouring water, and blew on the sparkles as they emptied onto the lens and grass.

The guards barely paused as the ground rumbled beneath them, continuing their march toward the children, even as the magnifying glass and the grass around it began to grow on the hill above. When the magnifier had grown large enough that the children could hide behind it, the guards' slow, waxy minds did not quite know what to make of this new development. They had not received instructions about giant magnifiers, so they just stopped dead in their tracks and stared at what they currently saw. The creatures before them now looked enormous through the great magnifying lens.

In the distance Diva shouted instructions, but she could not be heard over the rumbling of falling granite. The children saw she had picked up her skirts and was now trying to rush ahead, but her fancy dress and heels seemed to be slowing her down.

"Help me turn this," Eva said, wrapping her arms around the giant handle. The others leapt forward to help. "On the count of three, we turn it a little to the left to catch the sun! One! Two! Threee!"

They each held tight, slowly turning the glass until Eva shouted, "Stop!"

The effect was immediate. The sunlight caught the massive magnifying glass and produced a beam of heat down the hill. But the persistent wax men did not notice this new burst of warmth and light. What they *saw* was the children (and Leprechaun) had suddenly returned, so they resumed their journey up the hill, only to discover the effort was much harder without feet. Their bodies began drooping; their legs were the first to melt. Then the tan lumpy mass of their bodies began to spread into waxy pools, and when one melting guard touched another they stuck together and formed a single sticky mass.

This didn't seem to bother them a bit. In fact, they sighed gentle 'ahhhs' and 'ohhhhs' as they slowly dissolved across the grass.

Unfortunately for them, Diva must have been yelling "Get them!" or "Charge!" because the guards rushing out of the house continued marching up the hill directly into the path of the giant ray of heat, where they too suffered the same fate as the guards before them.

"Stop! Stop, you idiots! Can't you think enough for yourselves that you don't run straight into your doom?!"

Eva laughed. She was pleased that she had finally been the one to come up with an escape idea and use a tool from *her* pack.

"My mom always says, 'If Bobby jumped off the Empire State Building, would you do it too?'" Robert laughed. "Maybe this is what she meant."

"Uh, I'm not sure what an 'Empire State Building' is, but you're probably right," Reese nodded.

Just then they heard a thunderous noise erupt. "Uh oh!" Eva gasped, pointing to the stone house in the distance. "Looks like we made it out just in time!"

The crack in the stone tooth castle had finally given way and the house was completely breaking apart. Large stones fell inward, crushing the lovely interior. Some slid across the lawn in an avalanche toward Diva and the remaining wax guards at the bottom of the hill.

"My castle...." Diva cried, turning to the children and giving them the evil eye. "Ohhh! This isn't over! I will see you again! And *very* soon!" She reached into the bodice of her gown and brought out a small vial of Golden Luck.

"Look out!" Lauren shouted, pulling her friends to the ground.

But instead of using the Luck on them, Diva opened the vial and blew it on herself. It glimmered and settled on her in a cloud. Then she disappeared with a 'pop!' leaving behind only a puff of Golden Dust that settled to the ground like spent fireworks.

"Oh, my," Lauren worried, looking around them. "She just disappeared into thin air... Do you think she's gone?"

"You heard her," Robert replied, slinging his backpack onto his shoulder and turning to hurry up the rest of the hill. "She isn't gone for good, and I don't think we should hang around any longer to find out what she meant by 'very soon.'"

The girls nodded to each other and hurried after him.

15. Color Balls

When they reached the top of the hill, the children took a breath and looked around. They had a good view of the land and were able to get their bearings, though Lauren couldn't help looking back toward the remains of the house in case any of the wax guards were still coming for them... Or if Diva suddenly showed up, which, given their history, wasn't entirely implausible...

"Look!" Reese pointed. "The Tournament trail flags are down there by the woods! And one of the contestants is coming!"

They yelled and waved their arms, and when he got close enough to hear them, he looked up. They all stopped and stared in stunned silence. It was O'Sweeney. It looked as though half his bright red hair had been shaved off and he had large green bumps covering his chest and face. He stared at them for a moment before cackling, "Almost there. Yessir. Almost there, I am." He stuck his finger in his nose and when he pulled it out, he held it in the air. "North wind. Yessir. North wind." Then, with a twitch in his eye, he slapped at a bug that wasn't there and rushed on down the path.

"Oh, my…" Lauren whispered for them all.

"We still need a Golden Coin if we're going to get home," Eva worried aloud.

"He said he was almost there!" Robert said. "Do you think he was… uh…"

"Crazy? Probably. But that doesn't mean he wasn't telling the truth. Maybe the map can tell us more now." Reese reached to pull the magical map from her satchel.

"Is that your plan?" Lauren asked. "A Coin will take us home?"

"Yes," Reese answered. "But they're not Coins like money. They're special and they're only given to Tournament winners. We're all registered in the Tournament to win a Coin," she gestured to Robert and Eva, "and we *were* going to use one to rescue you and get you all back home. But here you are!"

Lauren smiled and reached for Reese's hand, "Thank you for helping Eva and Robert rescue me. You don't even know me but you've sacrificed so much to save me. I hope we can be friends."

"We already are," Reese smiled back, squeezing Lauren's hand.

"Gah, again with the sappy, girly stuff..." Robert moaned. "When you two are finished sharing love poems, can we get moving?"

Lauren stuck out her tongue at Robert's back

and Reese and Eva giggled as they started down the hill toward the thicket of dense trees.

"You sure live in a beautiful land, Reese," Lauren said, gazing at the landscape around them. "I *will* give Diva some credit – she picked a great spot to live."

"She'll live anywhere she can steal something," Robert grumbled.

"Probably," Eva agreed. "Wherever there's magic, I'm sure Diva will be somewhere nearby to get her hands on it..."

Reese frowned. "Let's just say that if she decides to try coming back here, I can arrange for her to meet up with a very hungry Troll."

"Whoah..." Eva said, suddenly pointing. "Look at that colorful field way over there. It sure is pretty!"

Reese squinted toward where Eva had pointed. "I think that's the last obstacle in the Tournament! Look!" She had been studying the now-complete map and she stopped to point at it for the children to see. "We can see the full course now. That means at least one contestant's finished the entire thing. It looks like if we'd followed the trail markers we'd have had to complete 20 obstacles before reaching this last one. I can't believe it!" She hopped up and down in excitement.

"Why didn't you just follow the map to begin with?" Lauren asked.

"Duh. It's a Magic map," Robert said simply.

Lauren blinked at him. "Of course it is..."

"If everyone had been able to see the entire map at the beginning of the race, we would have known to simply hike over this hill to reach the final challenge." Reese was still hopping up and down, seemingly unaware of Lauren's confusion. "But we strayed off the path to get Lauren and crossed over that hill instead of taking the trail around it! We missed all the other obstacles! The finish line is right after the field of Color Balls!"

"But isn't that cheating?" Lauren asked.

"Absolutely not!" Reese smiled, shaking her head. "The rules say the winning contestant has to reach the end of the course with the most Luck. It says nothing about completing every obstacle. Let's hope we have more Luck than the other contestant." She hugged herself with sheer glee.

"That's the spirit!" Robert hooted, jumping up and down with her. Then he stopped. "Hey, what are color balls?"

"The pretty field of color," Lauren sighed. "It looks like hundreds of flowers in a meadow."

"Yes, well those are *not* flowers, and trying to get through that field will not be 'pretty,'" Reese said, scrunching her nose.

"I don't understand," Robert said. "It just looks like part of the celebration for reaching the finish line."

"I'm sure that's what all new contestants think – if they make it that far. But if you've been around awhile, you know those tiny balls expand if you touch them. They stick to you as they grow, and if you can't get them off, the ball can grow big enough to suck a Leprechaun in and eat any remaining Luck right off them." Reese shuddered at this last part.

"Off their skin?" Lauren looked horrified.

"Yep," Reese nodded. "Not a particularly enjoyable process, from what I've heard..."

"Oh... That's horrible," Lauren said taking Eva's arm and rubbing at the Golden Luck.

"Ouch! Lauren, stop. It doesn't rub off – and you're *hurting* me."

"Exactly..." Reese nodded. "We're going to need a plan to get through there."

"Well, let's brainstorm as we go," Eva sighed. "We've made it this far, right?"

The children began their march toward the final event. Along the way, Reese told them funny stories of what life was like in the Land of Luck; how O'Sweeney had fallen into a pickle barrel at one of the farmer's markets and could not get the stink out of his clothes for weeks; how one year it was her mum's duty to provide a gigantic shepherd's pie for their annual Clover Climb, and one of the diners discovered her da's favorite slipper nestled between the mashed potatoes and peas; and the time a traveling salesman claimed that he had an elixir for sale which would attract Golden Luck Dust, and when several people had turned orange the salesman had disappeared, and the Town's Mayor declared a ban on the color orange.

"Why wouldn't he declare a ban on salesmen?" Robert laughed.

"Because everyone would be out of a job," Reese said. "'Everyone's selling something,' my da always says."

After about an hour of talking, climbing over rocks and fallen trees, and nearly swimming through overgrown clover, they were beginning to worry there was no way around the final obstacle. They had dismissed several ideas such as trying to create a wind to blow the balls away (too dangerous since they couldn't be sure where they would bounce) or using a massive stick to push the balls aside and form a path (Reese said the balls were smart enough to avoid sticks and poking at them would only make them mad).

"Hey, what about making ourselves slippery so they can't stick to us?" Robert asked.

"I don't think that'll work either," Reese groaned. "From what I've read, they stick to *everything*."

At last, the children stood in a clearing near the final stretch of the Tournament looking dejected and no closer to an idea of how to get past this final obstacle when Eva said, "Duh!" and slapped her own forehead.

"What? Duh what?" Robert asked.

"Reese's Dad gave us the answer!" she grinned "And you brought candy in your pack. There *must* be bubble gum in that stash you brought. I know I have a couple pieces in my bag *somewhere*. We can make our own balloons and float over the color balls high enough that they won't be able to reach us. Just like Reese's Dad tried to do over the acid river."

"That's a great idea!" Lauren clapped her hands.

"It *is* a great idea but we don't have enough Luck to make it across the field and earn the Coin," Reese said shaking her head. "I still have most of mine, but it isn't enough to get all four of us across... And what about the wind shifting again?"

Eva looked down at her Golden hands and then at her friends before turning to Reese, "*You* helped us rescue Lauren. We can use the Luck I have left to float us over the color balls so you can finish and become the leader of The Land of Luck. We don't need it for ourselves, Reese. You keep your Luck – you've shown real leadership helping us save our friend, and you deserve to win this competition."

Robert and Lauren nodded and grinned at

Reese.

"But... But how will you get home?" Reese worried.

The children gave each other a nervous look. "We'll find another way. I'm sure of it! We always do." Robert said patting Reese on the shoulder. "Now, let's do this!"

Just a short walk farther, they turned a bend in the marked path and could now hear a band playing from beyond the arch of rainbow balloons. Thousands of balls in all sizes and colors filled a space as long as a football field but wider than the eye could see. They were now close enough to see the other contestants who had made it to the final obstacle – and they were in bad shape. One had black eyes and his clothes were torn and covered in burn marks. The other sat at the edge of the field staring into an enlarged color ball, babbling to herself incoherently. The third... Well, the third contestant was *inside* a color ball.

The children looked away.

"Gosh... It didn't look this big when we were on the hill." Lauren gulped and plugged her ears in case the screams from inside the ball reached them.

"Hey, I don't have any Luck left," Robert said moving toward the color balls. "They won't care about me since there's no Luck to take, right?"

"Robert! No!" Reese grabbed his hand before he touched a ball. "They'll still suck you in... And pull off your skin trying to find the Luck!"

"Well then," he giggled uncomfortably, "Lucky break I didn't touch one."

"Gah! You big doofus!" Eva huffed at him, grabbing his backpack and pulling him farther away from the balls. "Let's just stick with the plan. So, look for some gum, okay?"

"You betcha. Gum..." he nodded, pulling off his pack and kneeling down to rummage through his supplies.

"Why can't they just move around

anywhere?" Lauren asked.

"Is it like the Troll Code?" Robert said, still pulling out pieces of gum.

Lauren looked bewildered, but Reese laughed. "Yeah, I guess it is," she said. "In every world there are rules. The balls can't move beyond the line because of the Tournament rules. I'm guessing magic of some kind keeps them contained. That's all I know. My da says *'Tis what 'tis.* I don't know why."

Finally Robert put down his pack and announced, "*Okay* then, each of us gets six pieces – and look at this!" He held up battery-powered, handheld fan as if it was a trophy. "We can use it as a propeller to help with the wind!"

"You brought a fan?" Eva stared.

"Nope. Your mom must've put it in my pack." He grinned at them. "Let's get to it."

Everyone chewed furiously. "Mmmy piece is ready," Lauren mumbled through her giant blob of gum.

"Mme tooph," Reese nodded.

Robert's mouth was so full he could only nod to Eva that he was ready as well.

Eva reached into her mouth and pulled out her wad so she could talk. "Now, everyone blow the biggest bubble you can, and then hold on tight with your lips. We'll need to hold hands so we stay together once we're up." The children nodded. "I'll make a wish for each of you, so your gum will hold you."

Lauren took her gum out and frowned. "What about you?"

"I'll wish for myself last," Eva said.

"I don't know... It doesn't sound like it'll work..."

Now Reese pulled her gum out. "The beauty of Luck is that when it's combined with a little ingenuity and a lot of good will," she paused, holding up her wad of gum, "it isn't so much Luck any more as it is... I don't know... hard work and destiny, maybe."

The children grew thoughtful.

"Alright, everyone. Reese has a Tournament to win. And I've got to be home by dark!" Eva gestured for her friends to put their gum back into their mouths.

They all nodded, holding hands as they began to blow giant gum bubbles. Large pink spheres wobbled and grew in front of their faces until Robert, Lauren and Reese had bubbles bigger than their heads bobbing around in their pursed lips.

"Just stomp your foot if you're ready." When they all stomped, Eva said nervously, "Okay, then.... Here goes!" She brought her wrist to her lips and blew on each clasped hand. Golden Dust swirled in a circle around her friends and landed gently on the bubble gum balloons.

Eva watched as each became more solid before launching her last speckles of Golden dust into the air. "I wish for a bubble that'll keep us in the air, and I wish for a wind that will carry us all there," she whispered and frantically started blowing the biggest bubble she could before the Dust settled.

Although her balloon wasn't very big, it was enough. The friends clamped onto their bubble gum balloons as tightly as they could while they held each other's hands, and slowly they began to rise into the air, up and up, over the tops of the hungry color balls.

It was difficult not to giggle with the success of their plan as they drifted toward the arch marking the finish line. Robert bicycled his legs lazily and used the fan to adjust their course as needed while Eva practiced Morse code by squeezing Lauren's hand as they floated.

Suddenly Lauren squeezed Eva's hand so hard she feared she'd lose her grip on her balloon. If she could have seen her way around the bubble, she would have shot her a stern look.

And then she didn't need to see to *feel* what

Lauren meant. They were losing altitude...

...and they weren't going to make it.

They were slowly descending... straight into the hungry field of color balls.

Magical Mystery Series

16. Floating Down to DOOM

The children began to struggle in midair as each realized they were not going to clear the eager color balls waiting for them below. They could almost see the edge of the field as their balloons began to deflate. Lauren's trembling chin threatened to force the bubble from her mouth when she heard the thrumming sounds of the balls vibrating just beyond their toes. An eerie "Yummm... Yummm... Yummm..." droned beneath them.

"Uhh!" Lauren cried, feeling Robert suddenly bob upward, her hand straining to hold on to his. Eva felt the shift as well, and when she rolled her eyes to the side, she saw that he indeed was floating a bit higher.

And *then* she saw the rain of candy falling from Robert's backpack. Oh, it was just like him to forget to zip it up! Eva fumed watching the precious candy scattering in the wind to the balls below. They would need it later for something, she was certain!

"Uoook! Uook!" Robert pointed down.

The girls stopped struggling and tilted their heads awkwardly to look where Robert was pointing. The greedy color balls had rolled toward the candy that had fallen from the sky, clearing a large empty spot in the field.

Robert pulled himself closer to Reese and turned sideways so she could reach his open pack. "Phhow uh andy," he grunted, which Reese interpreted to mean 'Throw the candy.'

Without having to say a word to each other, the team began to work together. Lauren held fast to Reese's coat so she could grab

Robert's backpack with both hands. Carefully tossing the candy farther and farther out in a large circle as they descended, Reese saw the color balls roll farther and farther away from the spot where they were about to touch down, noisily battling each other for the sweet treats.

Moments later when the group landed, they saw that they were really only momentarily safe. Even though they were mere inches away from the line that the dangerous eating blobs could not cross, they were utterly stuck. They were surrounded by color balls who would only be distracted until the candy was gone. And then what?

Robert spit out his now deflated gum balloon and carefully turned around to present his backpack to the girls. "Is there any more candy?"

"Yes," Reese said. "But not much."

"I'm sorry I teased you about bringing candy, Robert," Eva shuddered, squeezing closer to him. "Geesh, that was great thinking."

"Are we going to get mushy again?" he grinned. "Because this isn't exactly the time..."

"Everyone take some candy from the pack," Reese interrupted. "Let's see if we can make a path through the rest of these balls before they get any bigger."

Sure enough the color balls had already begun to grow as they absorbed the candy Reese had scattered – and as they grew, the small clearing became even smaller.

"Over there," Eva said pointing, "I think that's the shortest distance to where these things stop." They all huddled together and crept as one, toward the edge of the clearing. "I'm going to throw this piece and see if they go after it."

When three balls rolled toward the candy, snapping at each other and bumping other balls out of the way, Eva felt a little more hopeful.

"Hey! It worked!" Lauren clapped her hands.

"Let me try!" She launched a piece as far as she could throw, but instead of the nearest color balls bounding away to chase after the treat, the candy landed in a mass of balls already busily eating what had been thrown from above, while the nearest balls continued to snuffle and roll closer to the frightened group.

"Okay, uh…" Lauren looked troubled.

"I've got it!" Reese said. "Everyone get in a circle with your backs to each other."

The children obliged. "Now, everyone take one piece of candy. Got it? Okay, toss it – gently – juuust a few feet in front of you." The voracious color balls slurped toward the goodies, creating some space around the children. "Now let's move forward a few feet. Together!"

The children crept forward in a tight group, watching each other's backs. Above the humming in the field, they could hear a large crowd of Leprechauns gathered at the finish line; some shushing each other and some placing bets.

"Okay, toss another piece now," Reese spoke calmly. Next to her, Lauren was near tears and Robert looked like he had an itchy finger, desperate to toss the last of his candy and run like he had at the Troll Bridge. In spite of their terror, they did as Reese told them – carefully scattering another piece of candy and waiting for the color balls to go after it before they inched forward again as one.

Trembling, Eva said, "Why is everyone so quiet?" Every step the group made was met with a hushed "Ohhh!" or "Watch out!" as they inched forward through the dangerous blobs.

"Yeah," Robert said. "They sound like people watching golf…" He tried to laugh but found it wasn't that funny.

"Are we almost there, Eva?" Lauren said, "I can't see behind me. And I'm too afraid to turn around."

"Yes! I think we can jump the last distance."

"I sure hope so," Lauren said, "because this is my last piece of candy..."

Eva looked at her hands. One piece remained.

"Me too," Robert said.

"I've got two left," Reese said.

The crowd grew silent. They all knew that this story would be repeated for generations, until it became something of a legend. The self-assured, rogue Leprechaun girl, daughter of the land's best-known trickster, forming an unheard of alliance with two – wait, now *three* – human children... Well, it had never been done. Was this Leprechaun girl right? Would they all have to change the Leprechaun way and work together?

Reese drew in a big breath. "Okay, this is it," she said. The children nodded. "One... two... three!" Each of them tossed the last of their candy toward the growling color balls and waited.

"We're clear!" Eva shouted, watching the balls amble toward the treats.

"Run!" Reese called.

17. Finish Line

The circle disbanded and each of them raced toward the grassy clearing, jumping the last color ball in their path just as it sensed them. They landed and rolled, scrambling away from the invisible line that the dangerous balls could not cross. The wobbly color balls had greedily eaten the candy and were growing so quickly that the path they had cleared to the open field was now gone.

"That could have been us!" Robert said, sharing out loud what they were all thinking.

Color balls wobbled and grew and the children looked back from their safe distance to watch as the candy they'd tossed shrunk and twisted inside the glossy, transparent balls.

"But it wasn't." Eva grinned, looking toward the rainbow arch of balloons and the banner that read FINISH LINE!

The crowd just beyond the finish line broke into a roar of applause when Reese got to her feet. She grinned at the crowd waiting to pat her on the back.

"We started together so we should finish together," Reese said to her friends, holding out her hands to help them up.

The children stood and, grabbing hands, they raced forward laughing with sheer relief. Crossing the finish line together, they were surrounded by the crowd of well-wishers. A *Lucky Day Newspaper* photographer shouted to get their attention and bulbs flashed all around. Everyone talked at once, asking them questions about how they managed to finish the race.

"Did you know that only one other contestant has made it across the finish line so far?" a red-headed Leprechaun girl asked, hugging a blushing Robert.

"But no one's ever done it as a team!" Reese's father yelled over the noise, stepping out of the crowd and hugging his daughter.

The crowd pulled Reese away from her father's embrace, and she and her human friends were hoisted up; carried on the shoulders of the masses toward the large stage that had hastily been erected after the first contestant crossed the finish line. A band played, and many of the Leprechauns had begun to dance with excitement, linking arms and jigging in a way that made Eva laugh, for she and Lauren had danced that same way when they arrived home safely from their last adventure, with a basement full of Halloween candy!

When they were at last lifted to stand on the stage, they turned to face the other contestant who had made it across. It was a middle-aged Leprechaun who looked very tired and beat up. He was burned and bruised, and he had the same green spots on his face they had seen on O'Sweeny. There was a kindly older Leprechaun gentleman kneeling by his side, quietly telling him he had reached the finish line and that everything was going to be alright.

"That's the mayor!" Reese whispered, beaming at the others and pointing to the smiling Leprechaun in the formal clothes. He stood and smiled at them as he made his way toward a microphone on the stage.

"Ahem," the mayor said into the microphone. He motioned for the band to stop playing and the crowd fell silent again. "My fellow Leprechauns," he began.

"'T'were a thousand years passed since any contestant crossed the finish line," he waved behind himself, "with any spot o' Luck at all, and this year we've two! This brave gent, Nicholas, and this bonnie lass, Reese!" The audience cheered, drowning out his speech, until he raised his hands to quiet them again. "To finish the Tournament intact *itself* is an amazing feat o' bravery and a creative use o' wits. But 'tis perhaps the only year on record that we've seen contestants use collaboration." The crowd broke into loud applause as the mayor turned back and smiled at Reese and the children before speaking again. "As ye know, only a Leprechaun can become Leader o' the Land, so, I'm sorry children but I must disqualify ye." The crowd hushed after this last announcement, and by the expressions on some of her people's faces, Reese could see they felt differently now. After all, they had just witnessed a kind of bravery that only teamwork could produce. "Ahem," the mayor cleared his throat and continued. "Now, Reese and Nicholas, if ye would both kindly step onto the Luck-O-Meter, we'll measure the Luck ye have left. The contestant with the most Luck will be the winner and join the Council o' Seven as Leader o' the Land!"

Nicholas hobbled forward and the mayor helped him step onto the meter. The scale's bell chimed and the arrow climbed to 25% Luck. Everyone applauded as the mayor gently helped the contestant back down, where he once again stood facing the crowd with a dazed smile.

Reese slowly stepped onto the scale next. No sooner had her weight registered than the arrow bounced to 95%. Lights flashed, and alarms and whistles sounded until Reese, blushing bright red, looked around as if she wanted to run away.

18. Shave A Hen

The crowd stood in stunned silence. 95%? How was it possible?

The Mayor helped Reese down and spoke into the microphone. "Now, I've nary an idea how she's done it," he said, glancing at the gigantic Luck-O-Meter on the stage, "but this fine girl has, in fact, come through with more Luck than when she started!" The frighteningly loud contraption kept clanging "95% 95% 95%" until the Mayor pointed at someone to *turn that thing off, already!*

Reese dropped her eyes as the crowd broke

into wild applause. She tugged at the Mayor's coat sleeves, trying to get his attention, but he continued flipping through his notes with a pleased smile, unaware.

Finally, she could bear it no longer. As the children were hugging and the Mayor was waving to his townspeople, Reese stepped to the podium in front of him and took the microphone from its stand. "Um, pardon me?" The crowd went on cheering, knowing the speech which would ensue could wait a few minutes while they reveled, jigging and slapping each other on the back.

"Pardon me!" she shouted.

The mayor looked at her, startled. Even the children stopped hugging. Everything went silent as Reese looked across the crowd and gulped. "That's my girl!" Reese's dad shouted in the silence from somewhere near the back. She waved back at him with a pained expression.

"I, uh…" she faltered. "Well, I got some extra Luck along the way…"

"What d' ye mean, lassie? Are ye sayin the Luck-O-Meter is wrong?" the Mayor said, unsuccessfully covering the microphone with his thin hand.

"Yes! I mean no! I mean... I just want to be honest... I *took* some Luck from an evil ex-Tooth Fairy. That's why we've had the shortage. She had a pool of stolen Luck at her tooth house in the woods!"

"An evil ex-Tooth Fairy has been taking the Luck?" the Mayor quizzed.

"And she used fans to steal it!" Robert jumped up and down. "And her guards were ear wax!"

Eva kicked at him and the Mayor sighed, pinching the bridge of his nose and closing his eyes.

"Yes, but we – my friends and I – stopped her and released the Luck." Reese turned to address the crowd, "Most importantly, we did this *together*. Together we were able to free their kidnapped friend!" Reese turned and pointed at Lauren who gave a little, shy wave to the crowd. "And return our lost Luck!"

"Oy! What did she say?" shouted an ancient Leprechaun grandmother with a Lily Fern Fumble in her ear.

"She says they saved their friend from an ex-Tooth Fairy!" someone replied.

"They shaved a hen on the next boot dairy? Why would they shave a hen?"

"No!" another Leprechaun shouted. "They found their human friend – the one they came here for! Now shhh!"

"Well, well... T'was quite an accomplishment, young lassie," the Mayor said after a moment's thought.

"Yes it was. But I don't deserve to win this year. I *took* some Luck; I didn't earn it." Then she dropped her voice again and continued, "And I... I didn't go through the whole course..."

"*Now* what's she sayin?" the grandmother

shouted again.

"She didn't finish the whole course!"

"She didn't spinach the whole horse? Was that an obstacle this year? That's terrible!"

"She couldn't have 95% Luck!" someone shouted. "She cheated!"

The crowd erupted into chaos. Stealing Luck was a heavy confession. (Of course, it happened all the time, but to *admit* it – well, that was just *unheard* of.) But cheating on the Leadership Contest was worthy of exile!

"I want everyone here to learn from this!" Reese could hardly be heard over the noise. "My friends saved another human child and did a great deed for us all by joining forces! I want us all to become a society that works *together* and *shares* our Luck!"

Eva went to her friend and put her hand in Reese's. "I'm sorry," she mouthed and squeezed her hand.

Reese looked pale when the Mayor motioned

over two stiff-looking Leprechauns wearing dour suits and scowls. They turned away from the children and conferred over books and forms. The High Council spoke earnestly, poring over the manuals, pointing out texts, then shaking their heads or tapping their chins. At last, when the crowd was at its breaking point, someone yelled over the din, "Well, get on with it, will ye?"

The Mayor turned to the children and stepped directly in front of Reese. "My dear," he said gently, "I don't even think ye know how Lucky ye are."

Reese looked confused, but nodded anyway.

"The Council has made its decision."

19. Now I've Seen It All

The Mayor stood up tall and returned to the microphone. He raised his thumb at the sound booth and suddenly his voice boomed through the crowd. "My fellow Leprechauns," he began, "the Council has decided that our young lass, Reese, *has* earned the title 'Leader o' the Land.'"

The crowd simultaneously shouted, cheered, booed, danced and stomped on their hats. It was utter confusion. "It's the humans' fault!" some shouted.

"She did it for a noble cause!" shouted others.

"We'll have to change our ways now! This just won't do!"

"I can't hear a thing!" grandma laughed and danced a jig on her Lily Fern Fumble.

The Mayor spoke into the microphone again, "Please, please everyone listen. The lass might not've completed each and every obstacle, but from the sounds o' it she went through some t'were not on the course." He held up a rulebook and said, "There is nowhere in this text where it says a contestant must complete each. Only that one must cross the finish line with the most Luck. She endured some great danger and she solved our Luck scarcity *while* saving a friend. These are the qualities o' consideration, courage and honor this contest strives t' identify in its contestants. We applaud her for all o' these qualities and for her honesty. The Council feels Reese can teach our society a lot about working together." He turned to Reese and gestured for her to join him at the podium.

"Congratulations, lass! Ye are our next leader o' the Land o' Luck!"

Everyone was silent.

"Why is everyone so quiet?" Eva whispered to Reese. Reese looked like she was going to cry, but she walked toward the podium anyway and stood there with the biggest smile she could muster.

A smattering of polite applause broke the uncomfortable silence until the grandmother called out loudly, "What now? Did he say she was the next fender on a band o' trucks?" and everyone laughed.

The applause grew louder as the mayor patted Reese's shoulder and raised her hand in victory. The mayor leaned down and whispered into Reese's ear, "I think ye should make yer Golden Coin before our celebrations go any farther. What do ye say?"

She nodded and the mayor gestured for the crowd to be quiet. "Well then, please stand here."

Reese looked uncertainly at her new friends, who nodded at her and smiled.

Robert nudged her forward until she stood at the Mayor's side.

"Now, ye do understand that this victory is *yers*, aye? The humans aren't allowed to rule here, though they can be *honorary* Council members. And while 'tis a rarity, it has been allowed before. Ye've heard rumors from a Tournament many years past, I'm sure."

Reese nodded.

"Have ye seen a Golden Coin made before?"

Reese nodded again and looked at the ground.

"Well, then ye know it takes *all* o' us t' make the wish," he said smiling at her bowed head. "When I count three we'll collect the Wishing Breath and on 'three' ye stomp yer boot. Ye with me?"

Reese finally looked up at him and nodded, hardly able to breathe.

"Good. Is everyone ready?" he asked the crowd. Even the reluctant well-wishers seemed to sense the importance of Reese's victory and they shouted their approval.

"One..." The multitude of Leprechauns grew silent, drawing in their breath and facing Reese.

"Two..." The crowd raised their palms ready to blow.

"Three!" he yelled. Reese stood with her foot raised, watching, as if in slow motion, all the townspeople release their breath across their palms.

Released from bakers and builders and librarians; aunts and uncles and grandparents; tricksters and preachers and gardeners. Their breath seemed to pick up speed as it swirled into a fast wind, pulling the Luck from each one before curling toward Reese and spinning around her until all of the Luck that had covered her from head to toe drained from her and puddled at her feet onto the stage.

It all happened so quickly that by the time the Mayor's voice quieted its echo across the courtyard, Reese's boot met the Golden puddle. When she raised her foot again there lay a beautiful new Golden Coin.

"Ahhh! Fine job my dear," cried the Mayor. Reese stood before the crowd, stripped of all her Golden Luck Dust, clad only in the green tunic and leggings she started the year with. Her hat, somewhat askew after the long day, was now its normal hunter green wool, and her boots, slightly more scuffed, had returned to their original deep brown. "This is yer symbol o' office," the Mayor smiled. "Ye've now joined the ranks o' leaders o' The Land o' Luck." The crowd broke into cheers again at this last announcement.

"Wait..." Reese said, leaning down and picking up the Coin. "Wait, I don't want the Golden Coin."

No one in the crowd heard her over the shouting and applause, but the mayor stood next to her frozen in place, staring at her with confusion.

Reese reached out and took the microphone from his static hand and spoke to the crowd. "I don't want the Coin," she said and turned to face Eva, Robert and Lauren. The poor crowd became mute again.

"Oy! I've crushed my hearing aid! What did she say?" shouted the ancient Leprechaun grandmother.

"First she says she stole some Luck, now she doesn't want the Golden Coin," grumped another ancient Leprechaun. "Now I've seen it all."

"I'm bored..." a small child whined. His mother shushed him and continued watching the drama unfold in front of them.

"I want to give my Golden Coin to my friends," Reese said to the crowd. "They've been selfless and heroic and they need the Coin to get back home."

The Leprechauns began to mumble amongst themselves. *Was this allowed? Maybe she should give the Coin to the other contestant if she doesn't want it.* The Mayor rolled his eyes and waved the councilmen over for yet another conference.

"You don't have to," Eva said, stepping forward and taking Reese's hand.

"I know. I'm choosing to," Reese said pressing the Coin into Eva's hand as the crowd looked on, straining to hear.

"Wait!" Eva stopped short, lowering her voice. "My mom put a crystal in my backpack." The children stared at her. "We used a crystal to get here. Can't we use the crystal to make a rainbow and get back home?"

"Indeed," the Mayor laughed with relief. "We are Leprechauns, ye know. We've been known t' make a rainbow or two." He reached out and took the Coin from Eva's hand and put it back in Reese's palm.

The Mayor turned to Eva. "And now, my dear, perhaps it time you went home. May I have the crystal?"

The band, which had been waiting awkwardly for the sign, watched as the Mayor shook Reese's hand, and waited for Eva. They struck up a loud tune as the crowd cheered and began to dance. Even the ancient grandmother raised her skirts for a good jig.

"Reese, I guess we're going home now," Eva shouted over the celebration. "Thank you so much for everything." They hugged tightly.

"I'll miss you, Eva," Reese sniffled. "We could have been sisters... Aside from your weird ears, of course..." Eva giggled and wiped a tear rolling down her cheek, and while she did so, Reese secretly slipped the Coin into Eva's pocket.

Lauren stepped forward to hug Reese and said, "Thanks again for helping save me." Reese hugged her back and nodded, tears beginning to well in her emerald green eyes.

She turned to Robert who grinned and gave her a soft shoulder punch. "My middle name is actually Hugo..." he said.

She grabbed him and pulled him in for a hug. "I knew that. But you're still a hero. You're *my* hero." When she stepped away he was blushing.

Eva reached into her backpack and pulled out the crystal. She handed it to the Mayor who looped its silver ribbon around his fingers and carried it over to the Council. Then he held it up to the sunlight and each of the council members blew a little bit of Luck Dust on it. The crowd cheered louder when, instead of dozens of tiny rainbows flashing from the crystal, a single enormous rainbow arched down from the sky and touched the stage.

"I couldn't have done this without my friends," Reese said, wiping her eyes. "Come back and visit any time, okay?" She stood back.

Eva nodded, looking around one last time, as if to imprint everything in her memory, and saw the Mayor gazing at her.

"Thank you," she waved.

"Ye'd have made a great leader here too, young lass," he smiled. "Oh, and one last thing before ye go?" Eva nodded. "Tell yer mum, The Great Kathleen, Julian sends 'good wishes.'"

"Yes..." Eva barely whispered. "I will..."

The children looked at one another and stepped into the colorful arch of the giant rainbow.

20. The Family Business

Traveling home through the rainbow was much different than when Eva and Robert started their journey. Perhaps it was because they were not trying to fit into a tiny prism on the floor, or perhaps it was because they weren't going to need any Luck back at home, but this time the cyclone of sparkles did not stick to them, coating every surface of their skin and clothes with Golden Dust. Instead, the children experienced a rainbow slide much like the Great Pumpkin vine they rode to Fairy Land.

Instead of being scared when it felt like the
floor dropped out from under them, they
twirled down the slippery sides of the tunnel
whooping and laughing. "We're hooome!"
Eva shouted as she saw the tunnel open and

her house appear.

They each hopped from the rainbow when they neared the end, as if they'd just jumped from a swing while they were still high in the air, landing on their feet and racing toward Eva's front porch.

The front door opened and when Eva saw her mother's beaming smile and outstretched hands, she felt her heart fill with so much love she lost her footing for a moment as her throat tightened and her eyes filled with grateful tears.

"Good timing!" Mrs. O'Hare shouted toward them. "You made it home before dark." Then she squinted at the ground near the foot of the rainbow and said, "Eva! I think you dropped something!"

Indeed, glinting there in the grass as the day's light faded was a faintly glowing object. A Golden Coin!

"Mom! Mom, we did it!" Eva squealed, nabbing the coin and racing toward her mother's open arms.

"Indeed!" she laughed. "And here is Lauren, home safe and sound." She reached to pull Lauren into the hug. "I knew you'd do it. Welcome home, Lauren."

"Look, you guys!" Eva shouted, holding up the Coin and jumping up and down. "Reese must have snuck it back into my pocket!"

"Ahh, yes," Mrs. O'Hare smiled broadly. "You've been given a Golden Coin. I think you should put it in a safe place – these things can be terribly handy sometimes."

"Gosh!" Robert gasped, "She gave it to you anyway?" he squinted at the Coin, but Eva held it tighter.

"Why don't you all come inside, children." Mrs. O'Hare opened the door and the wonderful smell of dinner drifted out onto the porch. Suddenly the children realized how famished they were. "I've let your mothers know you'll be having dinner with us tonight."

"Mom, they knew you in The Land of Luck," Eva said, carefully putting the Coin back into her pocket. "They called you 'The Great Kathleen.'"

"Of course they did, dear, though that name is a bit of an exaggeration..."

"How do they know you? Were you there? How old *are* you?" Robert asked.

"Wait!" Eva clapped her hand to her mouth. "Diva! What about Diva? She wants our baby teeth and she said she was going to see us again soon! What if she kidnaps one of us again?"

Robert stopped doing his interpretation of a Leprechaun's jig and the children turned to look at Mrs. O'Hare with wide eyes.

But Eva's mom only laughed and ushered the children toward the kitchen. "Don't worry, children. You're watching out for one another. See how quickly you were able to get Lauren back home? Besides, she certainly won't be bothering any of you while you're under *this* roof."

Eva pulled her mother near and said quietly, "Mom? How do you know all this stuff?"

The Great Kathleen leaned down and put her hands on Eva's shoulders. "I know a lot because of The Family Business. But I *do* try to leave as much as I can to your father."

"The Family Business?" Eva looked confused. "Dad's a history professor."

Mrs. O'Hare laughed again. "He *does* know his history!" She paused and looked at her confused daughter. "Don't worry, dear. We'll always have plenty of time to talk about these things. That's one thing our family *never* has to worry about."

"But..."

"But not now," she said finishing Eva's sentence. Then she stood up and said, "I've made some homemade macaroni and cheese, and I need to get the chicken out of the oven. You kids go wash your hands now. Mr. O'Hare will be home soon, then you can tell us all about your adventures in the Land of Luck over dinner."

"Some of it wasn't Luck, Mrs. O'Hare," Lauren said. "Some of it was plain old regular help from my friends."

Mrs. O'Hare pushed a curl from her forehead and smiled. "Of course dear, I'm sure there were some Junior Detective skills involved as well."

The End

This ends the Magical Mystery Series: The Case of the Leprechaun's Luck

We hope you have enjoyed the adventures of Eva and her friends and that you'll join us again soon for their next adventure.

Please come and visit us at our website www.magicalmysteryseries.com for more information about the authors and illustrator.

While visiting the site please enjoy a sneak peak of our next book!

Coming in 2014!

A Magical Mystery Book 3: The Case of the Christmas Crime

In order to ensure the safety of Christmas and return the stolen magic, our heroes must once again battle Diva (and her Mom?!) to defeat the Snow Empire's evil plan.

Will our heroes be able to follow the clues and save the day while battling the abominable snowman and befriending an enslaved dragon?... all before their curfew?

Made in the USA
San Bernardino, CA
15 November 2013